Black August Revolution

Max Andrews

Cadmus Publishing

www.cadmuspublishing.com

PROLOGUE

"God is real!" Reverend Dean's voice sounds over the TV speakers and radio stations all across the country.

"I want to share a story with you about developing core beliefs. Not too long ago, a young man came and talked to me he told me that he beat a man have to death because he felt threatened. I asked him: What was the threat? He said that the last man that mean-mugged him beat him senseless, so he said to himself: 'If it's fuck me, it's fuck you!'

"This is a core belief, and when you continue to repeat this to yourself, you develop character defects: Coldness, callousness, manipulativeness, violence, etc. This is what you tell yourself after an event or trauma, to not feel helpless, or scared. It's all a mask, so when approached with the same or similar situation, we tell ourselves: 'If it's fuck me, it's fuck you.' This allows our character defects to kick in, violent thoughts, then our behavior strategy kicks in, assaultive. It's a progression of events. This is a core belief and how they manifest.

"When we continue to repeat this to ourselves, we live it out even in circumstances where it doesn't apply. Where does it apply? Nowhere. I'm not saying don't defend yourself. If we repeat to ourselves, 'Love Thy Neighbor,' we treat each other with the value of life and love.

"Some of us are broken, but we can heal. When we treat each other with love, we help heal each other. We can recognize a broken spirit and share that love. But if we continue to hold onto core beliefs that say, 'if it's fuck me, it's fuck you', we continue to live by that system of pain. We all have to ask: 'What are the core beliefs that we live by? Why do I choose this core belief? What character defects manifest from this core belief? How do I treat myself and others because of these core beliefs?' We do have more than one core belief, but if we have negative core beliefs, how we treat each other and ourselves is going to be negative. We are all human, we tend to have more compassion if we tell ourselves, 'I love myself.' You treat yourself and each other with that same love.

"I share this with you because the power of core beliefs is powerful. As a Christian, I believe in God's love and follow his teachings. I live in truth. Teach each other positive core beliefs.

"Ask yourself and the people around you: 'What do you do when someone wrongs you?' Hurt them in return? Your core belief is faulty. Here's a core belief to replace that. I'll read Matthew chapter 6 verse 24. 'For if you forgive men their trespasses, your heavenly father will also forgive you.'

"Your core belief is forgiving. Your forgiving a person who hurt you will come back to you. Let your core beliefs be God-fearing and loving. You don't have to be a Christian to have good core beliefs, but good core beliefs will be more powerful to you than money, for our character is what defines us and that comes from our core beliefs. God bless you!"

PART 1

Chapter 1

"Stop, get off me!"

"Shut up, bitch!"

"Get off my sister! Let me up!"

"Damn, this little bitch scratched me!" Nate yelled.

"Slap that bitch!"

"I'm going to call the cops! Stop, she's only 13!"

"I know you like this, the way you act. This is what you want," Darren says

"Darren, let's go!" Nate yells.

"Ugghhh," Darren moans.

"Please, just leave!" Megan yells

"Come on, let's go. Damn she scratch the shit out of you. You ain't fuck?" Darren asks.

"Nah man, let's just go before they call the cops," Nate says, pulling Meghan up off the floor.

"You want me to close the door?" Darren asks, while pulling up his pants.

"Just leave!" Megan yells.

"Morgan are you okay? Do you want me to call the cops?" Megan asks her older sister.

"Just wait for Mom to come home," Morgan says weakly and in shock, still lying on the floor with her pants around her legs and her face swelling up from where Darren punched her.

She wonders what he meant by, 'the way you act, you want this.'

'Did I want this? I liked him,' Morgan thinks as more tears run down her eyes.

She lays their confused while her younger sister comes out of the bathroom with a wet towel. She wipes down her older sister's face and pulls her pants up.

Chapter 2

SK, where you been?" the neighbor from across the street asks.

"I just got out the shower. It's hot as fuck out here. Why, what's up?" SK asks.

"You ain't heard? Your friend got raped. The cops are over there right now," Ron says.

"Who you talkin' about?" SK asks.

"The Mexican girl you always talkin' to. Kris paying us to help re-roof a house. We showed up, and 2 seconds later the cops showed up, so we left," Ron says.

"You sure? I just left her not even an hour ago. I'll be back. I'ma go call and see what's up."

"Hello?" SK says, answering the phone.

"I've been calling," Jimmy says.

"I was in the shower."

"You hear about Morgan?"

"I just heard. My neighbor came and told me. I'm about to go over there and check on her, see what's going on."

"Wait for me, I'ma go with you."

"Hurry up," SK says, hanging up the phone.

❖   ❖   ❖

"J, what's up?" SK asks, as they meet up and walk past the park towards Morgan's.

"I hope she okay," J says.

"I hope ain't no shit like that happen," SK says as they turn the corner.

"Look. The police still there. Look in the backseat."

"I see him."

"What you doing?" J asks shakily.

"Just turn around and keep walking."

"You're crazy!"

SK walks up to the police car, opens the back door, and starts beating the fuck out of this weird ass white boy.

"Hey!" the police yell, running from the front doorstep down to the car. He pulls SK out of the car and slams him on the ground.

"Get the fuck off me, you punk ass pig!" SK yells, while he is being cuffed.

"You have the right to remain silent...." The cop says.

CHAPTER 3

Its fourth down and end of the fourth quarter, with only two minutes left on the clock. The Kings are at the 28-yard line. The Hurricanes are putting up one heck of a defense against them." "I don't know, Chuck. The scoreboard says differently. The Hurricanes are favored to win. The Kings control the ball. I'd say the Kings have a good offense as far as right now, and a good defense. I mean, again, the current stats and the scoreboard say a lot. Maybe we're not watching the same game," Todd says, laughing.

"Here we go: They're in the huddle. I'm wondering what play they will come with," Chuck says rhetorically.

"So, what's the play?" Ansar asks in the huddle.

"Fake snap, straight execution. Everybody got it?" Kyle says, looking at his teammates for any questions. "Alright, break!"

"Here comes the down. You know, Todd, I miss three-point position: The thoughts of knocking my opponents to the grass just motivates me."

"Yeah, I hear you, Chuck. I do miss that part in playing defense. On the offensive part, the on-call strategy to outsmart my opponent and make the touchdown was and continues to be my biggest thing in all sports."

"Well said, Todd."

"Hut, hut, hike!" Ansar yells, trying to provoke the other team for a foul.

"Hike!" Sees it fails again, yells "Hike!" and the ball is snapped while the players rush to their new positions.

"Here comes number 14, Watt, smashing right into number 9, White, with his shoulder. Wow! That's a hard hit, and down goes the King's quarterback, number 12, Kyle Grant. It's a fumble and number 14 picks up the ball, blows past number 8, Smith. He's going to run it all the way!" Chuck yells. "Touchdown! 35 to 34!"

"Still no flag, and the coach is asking for a review," Todd says.

"And the touchdown is good!" Chuck says.

"That was one heck of a face grab, and the Kings quarterback still looks pretty hurt, there's only a minute left. Let's see what the Hurricanes do," Todd announces.

"If they do a field goal, it will be overtime. If they run it in, they'll take the game."

"The smart thing would be to run it. The Hurricanes haven't been the best in defense tonight. That last play was their best play and if they tie it they might not win. They run it, well the score will say it all," Todd says.

"Here comes number 42, Osmond Rice. He is one good kicker, but I just don't think that this is the best strategy. Ooh! It's a fake kick! He passes to number 16, Sanchez. Touchdown! 36 to 35! The Hurricanes will be celebrating tonight," Chuck says.

"Put the money in the bag. Hurry the fuck up! You think this shit a game?" The gunman yells at the Circle K cashier, aiming the gun at her head.

"Please, don't shoot me."

"Bitch, hurry the fuck up. You trying to get me caught by the police?" The gunman yells, cutting the cashier off.

"N-No." she replies.

"75 dollars, bitch? Bitch, that's all that's in there?" The gunman yells.

"I just emptied the register into the safe." She says.

"Where the fuckin safe at?" the gunman yells.

"It's in the floor, I just dropped it in there. I don't have the combination."

BOOM!

❖   ❖   ❖

"Dev, why didn't you block Watt?" Kyle yells, slamming his gym locker.

"Fuck you, Kyle. I told you don't go with that play. They know that formation: It's played out!" Dev yells back. "And what you think I wasn't trying to block you?" Dev says, still mad.

"Fuck you and the ref. I want to kill Watt for that shit. He fucked up, yanking on my face mask," Kyle says, still mad.

"Come on, Kyle, everybody else is gone. Let's get out of here and go enjoy the rest of our night," Dev says.

❖   ❖   ❖

'Fuck, fuck, fuck! Stupid bitch! Why she make me shoot her?' Tommy Gunnz thinks, frustrated.

"Come here, babe. I know it's not the kind of formula that you like, but it's all I could get. Where your mama at?" Tommy says, talking to his daughter.

"I see you got the formula," says an overweight woman, yawning and scratching her ass.

"Yeah," Tommy reply. "I don't know why the government won't allow you to get WIC. Have you tried to reapply?" Tommy asks.

"No, I have not, and I told you why they won't give me WIC. Get yo bum ass a job."

"Bitch!" Tommy yells.

"Who you calling bitch? Bitch ass nigga!" Tonya yells.

"I'm trying to get a job. It's hard to get a job at 16 with a felony," Tommy says.

"Well, nobody told you to be a felon," Tonya says sarcastically.

"I ain't got time for yo shit. Why don't you go apply for a job? I had to ask my cousin for this money to get our daughter some formula and all you got to do is get a job. You're 18."

"You know what, feed Kayla. I'ma go outside for some fresh air."

Man, I was 15 and got a possession for sales and I'm still being punished for it. I'm trying to feed my baby and can't get a job. Fuck it. I'ma get it how I get it,' Tommy Gunnz thinks to himself.

"Damn Kyle, this you?" Tre asks, as Kyle pulls up in a green Camaro on gold spokes. "That mothafucka hard!" Tre says, giving Kyle some dap, and saying how he needs to step his game up, getting a laugh from his young homie.

"How'd the game go… Never mind," Tre says, seeing the anger in his friend's face. "It's not the end of the world. You got talent. Sometimes you take losses."

"I'm not trying to hear it right now, Tre," Kyle says, cutting his friend off.

"Kyle, Kyle!"

A beautiful young sister runs up and hugs Kyle.

"Everybody saw what happened. That's messed up the ref didn't call that face grab."

"You always gotta hug me?" Kyle says, irritated and pushing Meeka off of him.

"Watt and his friends are here!" Meeka yells at Kyle's back as he goes in the house to grab a beer.

"Look who showed up. Ref, he grabbed my mask!" Watt says, making fun of Kyle.

"Fuck you, Watt. I'll beat your ass."

"You not saying nothing, lil nigga!" Watt popped off.

"Little?" Kyle says to himself.

"Kyle, let's just go. It's not worth it if you get in trouble," Meeka says, pulling on Kyle's arm.

"Meeka, shut the fuck up!" Kyle yells, yanking his arm away from her.

"Kyle, it's not worth it," Meeka tries again.

"You hiding behind yo bitch, Kyle?" Watt says, provoking him.

Bam! Kyle throws his left hand under Watt's chin, sending him backwards into a chair, knocking Watt and the chair over and embarrassing Watt even more.

Watt wrestles Kyle and they both fall on to the floor, rolling over and on top of each other.

"Police!" someone yells, as everyone starts running in different directions looking to get away.

"I'ma get you back for that, weak-ass dope fiend!" Watt yells at Kyle's back.

"Fuck you, Watt! I'ma kill yo bitch ass!" Kyle yells, as he's running out the front door.

❖ ❖ ❖

"You in trouble now." Boosie Bad Azz Blares over the speakers of the black-on-black Trans Am.

'Ima fuck his ass up when I catch him. Wish I would have remembered he was left-handed,' Watt thinks to himself.

❖ ❖ ❖

'Damn, I got to figure something out to get some dough. I turned in resumes. Shit. I got a trade, at least Camp did that much for me, but I still can't get no job.'

'Oh shit. That's what I'm talkin about. You always come through for me when I need you,' Tommy thinks, seeing this nigga with all this gold on. He looks again to see if anyone else is around.

"Yeah. This nigga is slippin," Tommy says out loud, as he walks up on the black Trans Am.

"Hey!" Watt yells, as he feels the cold still jammed into the side of his head.

"Nigga, shut the fuck up and give me your chain and empty your pockets bitch ass nigga," Tommy says in a hushed but deadly serious tone.

"Come on, man. I ain't got nothing," Watt pleads.

"Give me your money or I'ma blow your brains out."

"Fuck," Watt whines, reaching for his wallet.

"What you doing?"

BOOM!

"Fuck. Stupid ass nigga. Thought you was going to try and shoot me," he says, running down the street with his gun in hand.

CHAPTER 4

"What have we got here?" Detective Monroe asks the on-scene police officer.

"A 65-year-old black woman named Beatrice Gillard. Convicted for possession but has been working here for the last three years. One son and two granddaughters. Real polite, real good woman. Owner says she works at the post office by day, here during the evening to help her granddaughter through college."

"That's why she took on the evening shift, huh?" Detective Monroe asks.

"There's no video. Owner says the digital recorder broke two days ago and he's waiting on the replacement. There's no cash in the register. Only about three bucks in nickels and dimes," the cop says.

"No Witnesses?"

"None."

"What caliber gun?" Detective Monroe asks.

"We found a single 9-millimeter shell casing. I sent it to forensics to test for a print."

"You see that donut shop right there, across the parking lot?"

"Yep."

"Tomorrow, go see if they have a video surveillance."

"I'll get to it first thing," the cop says. "I hate seeing this type of shit. People getting their brains blown out over $30 or less," the cop adds in hoping the detective will talk to him.

"Notify the next of kin," Detective Monroe says, walking out the door and into the parking lot, leaving the other cops to do the rest of the work.

Chapter 5

"Shake it, girl!"

Monica was dancing and throwing her ass back at the man who had been hounding her friend for months.

'It's about time she hooked up with him. She's not as fine as she thinks, but you can tell he really digging her and as long as he good to her and her son, she don't care about much else. I hope he got a friend because I need a good man in my life.'

"Damn girl, you was throwing that ass back so hard, I thought you was having a seizure or something," Niesha says.

"That Tre song got me going girl, I'm not even going to lie. *That Bottoms Up*."

"How you going to hate from outside the club?" Niesha and Monica sang together, reciting Chris Brown.

"I wasn't feeling him at first. He just kept calling. At first it was just annoying, and I seen he's just real persistent. I just said, fuck it, let me see what he's talking about. Girl, I'm glad I did," Monica says.

"I'm glad you did too. You need someone who's into you not just for your looks. You can tell he digs you," Niesha says.

"I know girl, we going to see how it goes."

"Damn, Monica," Damien says, while handing her and Niesha a bottle of Alize. "I don't know how I ain't break out my pants the way you was dancing," Damien says.

"Shut up!" Monica says flirtatiously, hitting Damien in the shoulder.

"I'm glad you having fun," Damien says.

"I'm glad we are too," Monica tells him.

"So, where your man at Niesha?" Damien asks.

"Shit, I don't know. He said he was going to be here an hour ago. Shit, you got any friends you can hook me up with? Maybe a twin?"

"Shut up, Niesha. He's mine," Monica playfully says to her friend.

"I'm just saying, you never know what comes of asking," Niesha says.

"Well Damien, I had a great night and want to do it again with you sometime soon. You are funny and I haven't laughed like that in a long time, but it's getting late, and I need to get on to my son. He's probably driving my mom crazy by now," Monica says, giving Damien a hug goodnight as they exit the club into the parking lot.

"I really enjoyed my night with you. I knew I would, that's why I was so persistent. Maybe we can grab lunch sometime this week," Damien suggests, leaving the day open for her to choose.

"Tuesday?" Monica says.

"Okay. Do I call you?"

"How about 12:30? We meet up at Jimboys."

"Jimboys?" Damien asks.

"Yeah, Jimboys. I love their tacos and supreme burritos."

"Alright. Sounds good to me," Damien says.

"Alright," Monica says, giving him a hug and getting into her car.

"What was that? Good night and a dry ass hug? You better go back in and at least give him a kiss on the cheek," Niesha says.

"Damien, Damien!" Monica yells trying to catch up with him. She does and kisses him.

"Where that come from?" Damien asks.

"I don't know," Monica says, walking off smiling.

Chapter 6

SK, wassup bra? Njema ashabuhi," B Wax says, greeting his homie.

"Njema ashabuhi ku were ku," SK returned the greeting.

"What's them white people talking about?" B Wax asks.

"They gave me six months for beating his ass. The way the judge sentenced me, you'd think he got something against me," SK says, answering B Wax's question.

"You know white people into that weird ass shit, and your friend Mexican. You know they really don't give a fuck," B Wax says.

"The judge said he sent it to me like that because it's a hate crime. I yelled at his bitch ass and said, 'hell yeah, I hate that weird ass mothafucka!'" SK says, kinda heated while thinking about it all over again.

"Damn bro, you look like you're reliving the whole situation all over again. It's all in your face," B Wax says. "It's called resentment; you resend the same feelings over and over again every time you think about it."

"I'll be out soon, so it's all good."

"Look, I want to run something by you," B Wax says.

"Aight. Wassup?"

"I know you pretty smart and shit."

"What is it?" SK says, cutting B Wax off.

"I need some advice on how to get some money. I got this crystal, and the shit gas, but my packs kind of small. The Mexicans got some good shit. Not as good as mine, but they shit fatter," B Wax says.

"That's it?"

"That's it."

"Make yo shit fatter then, fuckin' nerd."

"I don't got it like that right now."

"Aight, look. Find out who brings the packs in and who they main hitters is. See if they'll do consignment and how much, and we'll holla tonight at dayroom."

CHAPTER 7

D*amn, six months for a hate crime. I just hope my friend doing okay. That's some fucked up shit to go through,"* SK thinks. As he lays back on his thin mattress, a tear rolls down his cheek. *'I need to smoke some weed, get my mind right.'*

POP! The loud lock on the door pops the door open.

"Wassup, bra. What's your name?" SK asks, as the newcomer steps in the cell.

"Kyle. You?"

"SK."

"What happened with you?" SK asks, getting to know his new celly.

"I didn't do it," Kyle says, as the tears start pouring out.

"You alright?" SK asks.

"I don't know, they charging me with two murders I don't know anything about. The police kicked in my door saying I killed a lady named Gillard and this kid named Watt. I don't even know who this lady is, but Watt…"

"You know Watt?"

"Yeah, he was on the Hurricanes. We played them the night before. After the game we got into a fight."

"Stop right there, bro. You see that speaker? It's a two-way, and they can use it against you, so be careful with what you say."

"I need help. I didn't do anything," he says starting to cry again.

He gains control and asks, "What about you?"

"I got 6 months for a hate crime."

"What happened?"

"I beat up some piece of shit who raped my friend and they called it a hate crime, so they gave me 6 months for it."

"Damn that's deep for sticking up for your friend. I hope she knows she lucky to have a friend like you, because that's deep."

"So, what are we going to do with this kid? We don't got nothing on him except that he got into a fight over a football game and there are witnesses that said they both threatened each other. From White's statement, they left the locker room around 7:45 pm."

"The shooting happened at approximately 7:20 p.m."

"The ballistics match," Detective Monroe says, cutting his partner off.

"There's no motive for this kid to rob or shoot Miss Gillard," Detective Ryan says.

"No, but he had motive to kill Watt, and the times match. They leave the party, and as they are leaving, he sees Watt, sees an opportunity, pulls the trigger. We use the approximate time the store clerk was killed, and things start tying in. Plus, we got ballistics. We tie him to both murders," Detective Monroe says.

"And White's statement about 7:45 pm?" Detective Ryan asks.

"We lose it and coach him that they left earlier," Detective Monroe says.

"This shit can't keep going on," Ryan tells his partner. "I'ma go along with it for now," he says as an afterthought.

"Of course, you will," Monroe says, walking out of the building. "Or I'll expose your ass. I'll lose my pension at worse, but you will lose everything."

CHAPTER 8

So, what's up with your new celly?" B Wax asks.

"Bra Smoove, fucked up circumstances," SK tells his boy. "You find out what I asked you?"

"Yup. Carlo is their main one. Vik is the one bringing in the packs and he'll front up to $500 worth of product and he'll give until the weekend to pay."

"Aight, look, we going to keep this amongst ourselves for now. Tell Vik to front the pack. We'll have it by Sunday afternoon and grab a couple bags," SK says.

"Also, grab a couple bangers. Once you get the pack, break it in half. We going to give half to the Bloods and keep the other half and bring them in on what we're doing."

"When will Vik give you the pack?"

"He said to holla at him as soon as I'm ready."

"Well, go get to it."

❖   ❖   ❖

"Vik," B Wax calls out, as he walks up to the Mexican area of the day room.

"What up, homie?" Vik says, thinking he's going to work this black addict.

"I'ma take you up on that offer. Just write down the number or whatever for me to send the money to and you'll have it no later than Sunday afternoon."

"You sure homie? This is a lot of product: $500."

"It's good, bra."

"Ok homie, is it clear?" Vik asks, making sure no cops are looking in their direction.

"You good."

"Here," Vik says, handing the crystal to B Wax with a grin, thinking he just got over because he only paid $50 for the whole thing.

"You got it?" SK asks.

"Yeah, I got it. It's pretty fat, too."

"Aight, go break it in half real quick."

"Aight, you got some plastic?"

"Nah, go rip some of the trash bag," SK says, counting all the Mexicans and white boys. 12 altogether.

'Yeah, they not going to like this at all,' SK thinks, smiling to himself. *'Oh well. Fuck em.'*

"Here bra. Here go half," B Wax says, handing SK the pack.

"Come on," SK says, walking away.

"Smack, what's good bra?" SK says.

"Nah nigga, I'm not fuckin with you, Skamz," Smack says, grinning, knowing somethings up with money involved.

"Damn, like that bra?" SK says jokingly.

"Look we put something together," SK says. "The eses got the dope on lock. They eating, so we got a pack on consignment. We know who they main man is and the nigga bringing in the packs. Instead of paying them, we're going to remove the main nigga and their mule," SK says.

"And what's in it for us?" asks Smack, smiling while his homies watch the conversation taking place.

"Here. This is half the pack."

"This nice, and this Vik shit?"

"Yep."

"So, the shit good?" asks Smack, knowing the answer. "When you want to go?" Smack asks

"Tomorrow morning at dayroom, we going to kick it off. We need y'all to assist us on the rest," SK says.

"Done. You already know how we function. Fuck them, wetbacks. No offense."

"It's all good, bra. Look, my boy hit his own shit, but the eses were just winning on the quantity of their packs. My boy's shit way better. So when we hit, he'll let you know so you all can re-up and we got to keep the Mexicans from getting anything in. If someone pulls up, then we got to knock him down and control the economy."

"Fasho," Smack says giving SK and B Wax some dap and heading back to where his homies are.

CHAPTER 9

POP, POP, POP, POP, POP. The cell doors open, and all the kids walk out, heading to their respective areas to meet and greet their homies. The Whites and Mexicans are on one side of the day, the Blacks and Asians on the other, and all the subgroups to their areas. Bloods in one area, Crips in another.

"SK, what's up bra? I got you a banger. Here," B Wax says, excited.

"Fasho my nigga. I'ma get Carlo, you take Vik. Cool?" SK says, to make sure they are on the same page.

"If that's how you want to do it, we'll do it like that."

"Aight. I holla'd at Smack at breakfast, so everything good. I'ma walk over and talk to Carlo. When I get off on him, you follow suit and get off on Vik. Then the Bloods going to jump in. Just make sure you get Vik good and get rid of your knife, then start swinging. Sound like a plan?" SK asks.

"Sound like a plan."

❖   ❖   ❖

"Hey, Carlo!" SK says, getting the ese's attention to come and talk to him.

"Hey, what's up? Do I know you?" Carlo asks.

"Nah. My name SK. I asked my peeps who I talk to if I got an issue with one of your homies. They pointed me in your direction."

"Ok, so what's the problem?" Carlo asks.

"Vik!" B Wax yells, getting his attention while SK talks to Carlo.

"What's up, Wax?" Vik asks.

"I wanted to catch up with you and let you know my people said the money will be there Sunday, but if they can, sooner."

"Okay. That's good homie," Vik says.

"Look to the boy with the big ass Sur on his chest. His real name is Michael Soto. He told on my boy. I got the paperwork in my cell right now."

"SK. Let me stop you right there. Understand our politics in our constitution: 'engaging the enemy.' We're not allowed to tell on 'our' people."

"I heard some shit like that. Y'all amended your Constitution actually. I have a copy of it. I needed to make sure that it wasn't a propaganda on y'all. But I need to know for the safety and security of our organization that this individual is not going to be in the building with us. I'm sure you understand where I'm coming from."

"I do, but I'm not in the position... ugghh.." Carlo gasps as the knife hits him in the cheekbone and again in the side of the nose. The last blow hits him in the cheek and chips some of his teeth.

As Carlo backs up, B Wax jams his knife in the side of Vik's head, behind his ear. Vik drops to the floor, unconscious, and the Bloods jump up and rush all of the Mexicans. The white boys pop up to aid the Mexicans. The guards start yelling "Get down!"

and begin using pepper spray on everyone in the dayroom. More guards rush in and immediately start coughing as they are trying to pull people apart. One guard gets put on his ass, knocked out by a wild punch he didn't see coming.

Some Mexicans are fighting, some are running. There is nowhere to go, they are just trying to get away. The white boys start yelling racial slurs while getting beat, kicked, and stomped. Two Mexicans get a Crip on the ground and start stomping. One guard cuffs up a Blood and two Bloods rush the guard. One of the nurses tries to pull a Crip to safety and falls on her ass from all the pepper spray on the floor. The guard's scuff up three Mexicans, while one of the guards cracks a white boy in the head with a baton, splitting his head open and knocking him out.

As the melee starts to die down, more guards rush in and pull the rest of the ones fighting apart. One of the white boys walks past a black guy laid out and cuffed on his stomach and kicks him in the mouth while yelling, "Fucking nigger! Hail Hitler!" Everybody not yet cuffed hops up and rushes each other for around two.

"Whoo. Got damn! This shit burn!" Kyle yells, laying in a puddle of blood and pepper spray, along with everyone else.

The police walk in with buckets of warm water and start dumping it on the inmates to get the pepper spray off of them, while laughing at the same time.

"What the fuck is your problem? Punk ass pig!" Someone yells.

"Y'all supposed to put us in the shower, not dump hot water on us, bitch ass mothafucka!"

The nurse yells, "These are kids!"

"These ain't no kids. They are monsters," the guard yells back.

"These are kids!" The nurse shouts. "Give them a shower or I'ma report it."

"How you holding up over there Kyle?" one of his homies asks.

"I'm good. That shit funner than football anytime!"

A couple of kids laugh at his enthusiasm. They all like the new kid: Telling him he a Rida and they going to put him on they set. Kyle smiles, liking the idea of acceptance.

✦ 25 ✦

Part 2

2 Years Later

CHAPTER 10

This class is the beginning of a lifelong career, and here we think black and white. There is good and bad; right and wrong. There's no in-between in pursuit of saving lives and protecting our communities. Our goal is to get criminals off the street and to keep them off the street. These people do not belong in society. In here, you'll learn the beginning of social justice: What is the law, why and how we enforce it, what is violent crime. This class is a way to be of service to others who want to live in a safe community. Some of you have been victimized, so you identify with the feeling. Some of you just want to give back to your community. Everybody is here for their own reason. You will all learn the same things, but you will interpret these things differently in pursuit of your goals and public service.

"My name is Curtis Ryan. I am a detective with the Elk Grove Police Department and a volunteer with the Youth Justice Readiness Center. If you have any questions, please feel free to ask. My partner, Kathy, is another volunteer and will be here shortly. Any questions? Yes, you in the white hoodie."

"My name is Steve. My dad was killed by a drug dealer. I'm here to learn how to enforce the law and get people the help they need; like making sure they get substance abuse treatment and anger management and make sure they get the rehabilitation—"

"Let me stop you right there, Steve. The word rehabilitate is a trigger word for me. Criminals do not rehabilitate. They only get smarter and manipulate and system. That's why there's such a high recidivism rate."

"I disagree with you. You are extremely closed-minded and have thinking distortions. My dad went to jail for murder. When my mom told him she was pregnant with me, he never committed another crime again. He said he had a paradigm shift and committed himself to being a father and a husband. He told me he took advantage of the self-help courses and that they really helped them grow"

"What's your name?" Ryan asks, thinking she's going to be a problem.

"Kelly Pars."

"Why are you here Kelly?"

"I'm here to learn how both sides of the law work: The criminal justice system and the rehabilitative system, with the pursuit of local politics, proposing new laws in rehabilitative efforts."

"That's very good Kelly. I'm sure you'll learn a lot from this class and will be able to make a lot of changes in our justice system." Ryan Says.

"I know I will," Kelly says sarcastically, not liking Ryan.

"Any other questions?" Ryan asks.

"Hi. Sorry I'm late," says a beautiful brunette. "My name is Kathy. I am the other volunteer with YJRC. My car is battery died, so please don't think this is an everyday thing."

"Kathy, I've already given them the introduction, so we can go ahead and hand out the packets and have them answer the questions and get started," Ryan says.

'Damn, she's beautiful,' Kathy thinks, locking eyes on the caramel skin Mexican girl.

'*She's fine,*' thinks the Mexican girl, wondering if she likes women.

She looks familiar Kathy thinks. A young Jennifer Lopez crosses her mind.

Chapter 11

What you reading?" Kyle asks.

"It's about economics, comparing other countries conditions and economic policies, example, a lots of people say they don't have the same work opportunities but what kind of work opportunities? Lights Arizona and Mexico, the only thing different is economic policy. Yuma, Arizona is right on the border, it's storming housing, jobs, etc., it's the same climate, vegetation, same environmental riches nothing different from their neighbor Mexico. The differences is there's a border between them and each country has different economic policies which insurance Define opportunities. You control economic policy, you control opportunity."

"That shit deep why you reading that?"

"I've been studying economics, most of the books you've been seeing me read all that time that's what that is. I like economics. I've been wanting to own my own bank since I was a kid, that's why I've been studying."

'You beyond your revolutionary thing.

"That's because I'm against unjust laws."

"Hold on if you just against unjust laws you can just advocate for more fair loss, revolutionaries are against the whole government, communism is a form of economic policy, if you want to learn that we can study, that ain't nothing."

"Ain't you on your revolutionary shit?" Kyle asks.

"Kind of, I believe in Democratic socialism, I just think there are definitely better ways to run the government then what the US is currently doing, plus I like capitalism or the making of capitalism." SK says smiling.

Chapter 12

I feel you, bra. Look how these people doing me. I want you to see how these white people doing me. They put racism in the game. They divided us by using racism to separate us. He's White, he's Black, he's Mexican. I need to break that cycle of thought and vocabulary. Look, I've been fighting these two murders for two years; something I ain't even do. You about to go home on something you did do. We know what happened, but they don't. Dude ain't even tell him they just said you stabbed him. No witnesses, no fingerprints on the weapon, the pig just said he seen you throw a weapon, and that's a lie. But the goal is to keep us locked up, that's it!

"And that's one of the things I'm against, Kyle. You and I see this firsthand. They lock us up and don't give us no help. There are people in here that need serious help. Like look at ol boy. He was a 16-year-old male prostitute. He was telling me his story, some sick shit, that's some serious trauma. He need therapy, not getting thrown in here."

"I was going to ask you about that. I heard y'all talkin. How did he get arrested?"

"The police arrested him because he wouldn't fuck em."

"What? Hell nah! That nigga lying!" Kyle says.

"Nah, he telling the truth. He been fuckin em, they would just let him go instead of arresting him whenever they caught him. Shit get deeper than that."

"Damn SK. Nigga really told you that shit. Shit make me want to kill these punk ass pigs!"

"Let's hit this dayroom, I'm trying to call my friend."

"SK, real quick what got you into dealing dope and all that?"

"Poverty, and I justify it with material dialects and using it to help create the change I seek."

"Why are you so angry?"

"You want something to cry about? I'll give you something to cry about. Before the giant palm slaps me across the face," SK has a sudden flashback.

"What's up?" Kyle snaps him out of it.

"Nothing bra," SK says, not wanting to talk about it, hating the thoughts of being helpless again.

"My bad. I shouldn't have even asked."

"It's good bra!" SK says wondering if he saw the look on his face.

CHAPTER 13

Morgan, I am sorry. I know it's hard, he was still a part of you. He's my nephew, it's hard for me to get over it. It hurts me too to sit here and watch my sister get raped and not be able to do anything. It's done something Morgan. I just don't think you had to put him up for adoption."

"Megan, I couldn't raise that baby. I think of that baby, I think of that day, so please stop!" Morgan yells, showing more anger than how she really feels, wanting to cry but not wanting to show weakness. "I hate men, and SK, why he have to assault him? They are all monsters!"

"Morgan." Megan says, seeing the demons in her sister's expression. "I love you and I wanted to let you know I seen J. He told me to tell you hi, and SK-"

"Shut up!" Morgan yells.

"Morgan, you don't get it. It's like you hate men because of one person. Not all people are the same, not all men are the same. You are not a victim, don't let that label define you."

"You a psychologist now?" Morgan says with venom.

"No, you're my sister and I see the hate and I know that's not you. You are hurt, so am I, but hating men isn't the way, and SK loves you," Megan says, walking off.

"I just hate he wasn't there when I needed him."

'He deserves to be locked up,' she thinks, automatically rejecting the first thoughts, feeling her anger come back and justified in her hate. Kathy is right, men are pigs.

Chapter 14

Tip, what's up lil man?"

"Who you calling little? You the one with the peanut head," the 9-year-old jokes, running off with basketball in hand.

"Nick, what's good? Yo lil man a bad ass little kid, little dude got jokes. He called me peanut head."

"You telling on my son?" Nick says, sticking up for his son.

"Now I see where he get it from. How you been though?"

"Same shit." Nick says, watching his son shoot hoops, hoping he chooses sports over the streets.

"Nick, tell me something good."

"Dragon, I'm done. I'm not going to continue to do the same shit over and over again, hoping for different results. I sell dope, I get pulled over, I sell dope, I go back to jail. I need to do something different."

"Sell guns then."

"I'm done."

"You ain't never done," Dragon says, looking at Tip as he makes a layup. "This what you signed up for. When you was doing bad, you turned to us. Don't forget that!"

"What you need me to do?" Nick asks, thinking about how Dragon looked at his son and thinking about how to get Dragon away from his house and kill him at the first opportunity.

"We got ten keys of black. We want 100 bands back."

"We got out to all of the parts of this organization. We all play our part and it's more than just me," he adds as an afterthought, knowing his message was sent.

Chapter 15

B abe?”

“Yes Damien?” Monica says drawing out his name playfully.

“I am glad that we adopted Nate, he brings an added joy to our family.”

“He does what makes you say that?” Monica asks.

“I was thinking about how I was adopted and not really feeling loved. I love Nate like he’s my own son and he brings me more joy knowing how much I love him, and it makes me appreciate my parents more because I always had doubts like how can someone love you that’s not a part of you? I just didn’t think you could fully love like that.”

“Well, you didn’t birth me or Josh, I know you love us.”

“I just thought it was a different conscience, adopting.”

“You love me, right?” Monica asks.

“You know I do!”

"I love you too." She says, smiling, loving the decision she made to marry this man, and knowing he loves them.

Chapter 16

Juju what's brackin blood, where da bitches at?" Killa asks. "Sup wit my nigga?" Juju says, embracing his homie. He looks him up and down, "Blood you fuckin around? You look skinny as fuck."

"Yeah bra, I've been hitting the powder." He says, letting his index finger brush over his nose. "That shit be having me on one blood, battling demons, shit get me in the zone."

"Damn, my nigga." Juju cuts in, "that shit ain't smooth, I feel you on getting high, I'm not knocking it, but that shit got you looking all kinds of fucked up."

"Nah, I'm good nigga. I just need to get some sleep I'll be alright. Where everybody at?" Killa asks wanting to change the subject.

"Niggas around." Juju says, not really wanting to tell Killa anything, knowing people change off of that shit.

"You hear about your cousin?" Killa asks.

"Nah, what happened?"

"Them crab ass niggas shot Don- Don house up, blood got it. This was probably about 2 hours ago."

"Nigga he'll nah." Juju cut them off.

"On Bloods, they lit the whole house up, blood was sitting out on the patio when it happened."

"Blood you was there?" He asks, not really sure if Killa was giving him accurate information.

"I was walking up to blood house when I bench the corner there was hella police there. I asked the neighbor what happened. Smoker Mike was cross the street he seen me, came over and told me what happened."

"Blood why you ain't call?" Juju asks heated.

"Blood I'm not going to get on the phone and say shit. You know the K9 on the whole hood." Killa shoots back.

"Blood why you walk up and ask about bitches? Who does that? That shit got you fucked up. Get the fuck away from me weird ass nigga." He was mad that his cousin got shot and this bitch ass nigga asking about bitches.

"Blood fuck you nigga! Talkin to me like that!" Killa yells.

Juju socks him in the temple, putting Killa on his pockets.

"Bitch ass nigga!" Killa shouts.

While trying to get up, Juju kicks the shit out of him, he balls up in defense, waiting for the opportunity to get up. The neighbors look on and start walking inside their houses. Juju kicks Killa in the head and knocks him out.

Chapter 17

Wat's that's about blood?" Ryda asks, seen what just happened.

"I know you ain't levelheaded dude, so I know it was something."

"Look blood." Juju says, re dialing his cousin's cell, he hangs up and calls again, gets voicemail and stops trying.

"Look blood this nigga conies over here high off dope, asking where the bitches at, then tells me shorts got shot, something about Don-Don. The Rip's shot up his house and Short was on the patio and got hit."

"You call Don-Don?" Ryda asks.

"Yeah, blood and Short both not answering."

"Why would blood ask about bitches then tell you about Short? Blood need a D.P, that's a breach of security, I'm not letting niggas know, on me bra got a D.P coming. Me and Cam gonna D.P blood. Niggas going to agree with that off top." Ryda says, feeding off Juju's energy.

"Fuck blood." Juju says.

"We need to find out what's happened, see if Short and Don-Don aight, and see what they want to do, soon as we find out who pulled the trigger we'll rock, and they can ride when they ready." Ryda says

"It's crazy cause we don't even beef with no Crips even despite the fact they Crips. It's got to be something, and I can't think of nothing."

"Stop thinking. Wait till we get the facts, we'll go from there." Ryda says.

"You right bra. I'm just scared this shit might be true. I need an outlet."

Chapter 18

That was a good idea, I'll give you that. Those fuckin I niggers won't even think twice about it." Says Wacko.

"We need to take over the whole area, they got all the malls, stores, hella traffic running through there. It's too much money to pass up. Those fuckin niggers don't even know what to do with that kind of shit, all that money."

"So soon as we clear the blacks out of that area, I get my membership?" Rudy asks just to make sure nothing, knowing how people's politics are.

"You good. You'll make member, just keep doing what you doing, you got a lot of support." Wacko reinsurance him.

"So, what are our friends at the police department saying? Wacko asks.

"Devil said he'll arrest the shooter as soon as his informants gets him the information, it's all lined up, he told me the informants is a white nigger, name Collins and that Collins got some smut on him. He does us the favor of locking up the shooter, we take care of Collins."

"And how do you plan on doing that?" Wacko asks.

"I'll tell the Crips I got in inside connect and give them the paperwork that's Collins snitching and let them continue to do our Dirty Work, and while the Bloods and Crips wipe each other out and fight amongst themselves, we'll move in and start setting up shop."

CHAPTER 19

"Cuz, you see the way that you see the slob ass nigga chest story Spurtin blood? That's the only blood I like." Duce says full of himself.

"Nigga shut up." Ducc says, nervous and high off the coke.

"Nigga how much them wetbacks pay you?" Crip face asks. "We might need some attorney money, just to be safe and cover all avenues." He adds in, while snorting another line of coke.

"Them niggas ain't pay no money, only 2 lbs. of Coke." Duce says.

"Nigga we got to go out of state and get some dough. We can win O.T, plus it will give us some time to let shit cool down, the police going to be out in the Bloods going to be Trippin on Short getting shot, that's one of they main niggas."

"On everything." Ducc says, cutting Crip face off. "Nigga get points for that." Liking the idea of being acknowledged. Damn, where that thought come from. Ducc asks himself, thinking back to being a kid in his parents never acknowledging him when he did good, only scolding him when he did bad. "Damn, I'm still acting out for attention, nah, this powder got me trippin." He says out loud, snorting another line to try to suppress those thoughts that had been repressed all this time. "Yeah, Crip face right, let's go out of town and let shit die down."

✦ 49 ✦

CHAPTER 20

Blood, what happened?" Juju asks Don-don in the hospital hallway.

"Not here." Don-Don replies, "let's go outside I need a smoke anyway." He says nervously, looking around at all the police waiting around for Short to get out of surgery and question him.

As they walk out, stay walk past the police who lock eyes with Ryda and smile.

"What the fuck you smiling at?" Juju yells, "You think this shit funny?"

The pig chuckles, places his hand on his gun and tells him to calm down.

"It's all good." Ryda says, "My man just upset, I'll take him outside to get some air and cool off."

"Sounds like a good idea to me." Detective Monroe says, laughing at Juju for being so stupid.

"What the fuck was all that about?" Juju asks, yelling at Ryda, like he suspect, suspicious of everyone right now.

"I don't know what the fuck that pig smiling at." Ryda says.

"You need to get ahold of yourself."

"Look Blood, don't tell me what to do." Juju pops off, no knowing Detective Monroe's seed had already been planted.

"So, what's happened blood?" Juju asks Don-Don.

"Look, I was inside when the shit went down. I laid on the floor as the bullets came through the window, I started to call to the front door, I seen a spurt of blood then Short fell off the chair clutching his chest."

"And you ain't see no car or nothing?" Juju asks sarcastically.

"Three people in a blue Camry."

"Duce." Juju says out loud.

"Who?" Don-Don asks.

"Duce. Duce got a blue Camry, but it don't make no sense. Why would he drive his own car?"

"Aint no telling, people do dumb shit all the time." Ryda bust in.

"So, you sho it's Duce?" Don-Don asks.

"I'm sure bra but we don't beef with them niggas so why just shoot your pad up?" You not telling us something?" Juju says, more of an accusation then a question, looking to get more answers.

"Nah blood. I can't think of nothing."

"Think on it blood, see if we missing something, we going to ride regardless but we need to see if there is more to it." Juju finishes, then walks back into the hospital.

CHAPTER 21

"SK, you getting out tomorrow huh?" Audi asks. "Yeah, it's been too long ass years, I was only supposed to do for months. My dumbass turned it into a term, I'm ready to go, I ain't even had no pussy yet."

"You going back to of girl?"

"Who's that?"

"The one you in here for?"

"Nah bra, you good though?" I'ma go work out." SK says walking off, hurt thinking about his friend. "She ain't even wrote me and people saying they've been giving her my messages, every time I ask about her people get quiet or change the subject."

"J.D. what's up you trying to work?"

"Come on spend some time with your boy before you go." He says, folding up his t-shirt and setting it down on the hot ground to put his hands on for the push-ups.

"You ready?"

"Ready."
"Anzi."

Chapter 22

S hort dead." Juju thinks to himself, shedding a tear, "I can't even trust these niggas. This nigga Don-Don lying about something, this nigga Ryda what the fuck was all that shit with the police. Who the fuck gonna crawl to the door while bullets flying and there's nothing to cover you? He going to have to come better than that. Niggas not just going to start shooting our house is up for nothing. What are we missing if Don-Don not lying? Am I overthinking this shit?"

"Hooooonk!" He says hand out the car window to waive the car around. "Damn punk ass bitch you don't got to mean mug and shit."

"Damn I don't even recognize myself in this mirror, bloodshot red eyes, cracked lips, sunken face. I can't wait to find these niggas."

CHAPTER 23

Blood, what the fuck happened over there? I can tell by the look on Juju face, he don't believe for one second that them bitch ass crabs shut your pad up for no reason."

"Hold on." Ryda stops Don-Don from interrupting. "Juju don't buy it either, you're not telling us something or we missing something. Juju thinking on it, you seen it, I seen it. What are you not telling us?"

"Look, I told you I was coming out of the bathroom, they just started shooting, I got down and crawled to the door so I could bust, by the time I got there they had pulled off. I don't know why they shot my pad up. Shit don't make sense to me, and I'm being looked to make sense of it."

"You fuckin one of they bitches, or something?"

"Nah I been fuckin wit Jessica, that's it."

"I don't know blood the funeral Wednesday and I know Juju, I wish he'd answer the phone so I could holla at him, so we could slide on them crab ass niggas for that shit."

"He not fuckin with you either after the way the police looked at you, smiling like he know you. Something you not telling us. Trying to breathe on me." Don-Don thinks as his inferiority complex kicks in.

CHAPTER 24

SK, I'ma miss you, bra."

"I'll stay in touch with you and send you some books and shit to read. Continue to stay strong in your education and political beliefs, more importantly don't give up on God. I'ma go holla at your mom and send you some pics."

"I know you going to, that's why I fuck with you. I got hella love for you. You are a good dude all through. I know how shit be, but truly hope you never come back to this shit."

"Me too, I hope to see you soon out there with us. Maybe you should give Meeka a chance. She really likes you and ol' girl ain't doing nothing for you. Meeka steady with the letters, just consider it, give her some time, a few more letters I bet you get her on the right track politically, she'll be good for you. She'll be shouting Revolution before the year's up." SK says and Kyle starts laughing.

"Aight bra, imma be at you shortly." SK says as he walks out of the cell into the dayroom.

"SK be cool bra. Smoke one for me."

"SK, tell B Wax look out for me. Be smooth."

"Name one of them newborns after me."

"SK, cuz tell Young to look out and stay focused."

"Yall be smooth." SK says, walking out of the door into the hallway towards the parking lot.

As the double glass doors closed behind him and the Sun beats down on him, from the other side he finally understands what people mean when they say that air is different. It's all of the oppression lifted off of you. The crisp air brings a renewal to your spirit, your vision sharpens, the mental vision widens. "Thank you, Allah!"

"Let me not forget my hardships, let them not Define me but strengthen and add to my character."

"Hey brother, meet your niece." SK's sister says, handing him his niece to hold for the first time.

"Hey niece." He says, looking at her for the first time ever and thanking Allah for another Blessing.

CHAPTER 25

THE FUNERAL

Today we mourn the loss of Sean Marks, known by his family and friends as Short. I didn't know Sean personally, but I know his mother and through her I got to know Sean.

"I'm going to read Revelation 1 verse 7; Behold he cometh with clouds and every eye shall see him and they also which pierced him and all kindreds of the Earth shall wail because of him. Even so amen.

"I share this particular verse with you to say he will come to us all and they also which pierced him every eye shall see him. Every eye. When you look into the mirror what do you see? You see what you want to see but how does God see you? Because that's how we are measured, not by how much money we have but what we do with it, not by how many people we know but how we treat them, knots by how much influence we have but how we use it.

"Matthew 24 verse 36; No one knows, however when that day and hour will come, neither the angels in Heaven nor the son. The father alone knows.

"I say this, we must be vigilant in our hearts and actions not betraying our brothers and sisters to falsehood and what I mean by this is don't encourage each other to Greed, lust or violence. We must not betray ourselves to these things. Look what happened to Judas, he betrayed Jesus because he betrayed himself for a few coins, for corruption was in his heart. Judas never got to enjoy those coins.

"Acts 1 verse 18 and 19; with the money that Judas got for his evil act, he bought a field where he fell to his death. He burst open and all his insides Spilled Out. All the people living in Jerusalem heard about it and so in their own language they call that field, Akeldama which means field of blood.

"We know the story of Sean's death we know his life was betrayed for greed and we know through the Bible what happens when we betray our brothers. All throughout Revelations it teaches us of what's to come. If you notice most of these things come from the sky. Again Revelations 1 verse 7, behold he cometh with clouds... We don't know when this day or hour will come but how are we preparing for our judgment with our creator.

"We can follow Sean's example even though he may not have, he kept a Bible at his bedside and spoke to the kids from it. He was known for quoting his favorite scripture 1st Peter chapter 3 verse 8; you must all have the same attitude and the same feelings, love one another and be humble and kind with one another.

"This is a building block and why Sean's life is memorialized as a pillar in our community. Lead by example as Sean did. I'll let his mother speak now. God bless."

"Follow the green Lexus." agent Howard tells his colleague as the white Durango pulls off two cars behind the Lexus, a blue sedan pulls off behind the Durango.

"Why are we following the Lexus?" Agent Phillips asks.

"Because I want to get a bigger picture of what these guys are doing. We know the blacks and Mexicans got something going on, but what? We know it's more than just guns and otherwise we wouldn't have called you guys in on this." Howard tells his partner. "We need to follow up on some leads. These two just followed up with the Mexicans and they just met up with the Bloods. We need to know what organization they belong to. We know they sell guns; we know the Mexicans got drugs, but the blacks haven't done any drug transactions with them."

"Boop! Boop! — Boop, boop!"

"Why are we pulling them over? We're only supposed to monitor searching activities as of right now."

"Just pull up behind them and follow suit."

"Step out of the vehicle!" agent Howard yells. "Put your hands on top of the hood. Feet apart!"

"What the fuck is going on? Why you punk ass pigs harassing us?" Cash asks heatedly.

"Where the guns at?" Howard yells in his ear, shoving his gun into the side of his rib cage. "Look, shut up and tell me where the money and the guns at or I'm going to find a reason to shoot you!"

"Look man, I don't know what the fuck you are talking about."

"Hey! Hey!" The driver yells as Phillips puts him in cuffs.

"Howard what the fuck are you doing?" Phillips asks.

"Putting him in cuffs. Set them both on the curb and tear the car apart."

"Hey what the fuck y'all doing?" Cash yells as the FBI and ATF agents rip their car apart.

"Look here!" Agent Howard yells. "Loaded 9mm under the passenger seat."

"Fuck!" Nickle says under his breath.

"Hey Howard. I got a duffel bag full of handguns and a couple of silencers."

"Zip it up."

"Zip it up?"

"That's what I said."

"Can I talk to you for a minute?" Phillips asks.

"What we doin?"

"We're doing a search and seizure."

"We had no probable cause plus we are only supposed to be monitoring them."

"Look, I'll let y'all go, tell me two things or go to jail for transportation of firearms and whatever conspiracy charges I decide to trump up."

"Where's the money and why are you doing business with the Mexicans? Think about it."

"The money inside of the backseat."

"What the fuck." Nickle yells as Cash tells the Feds where the money at.

"Fuck it! I can't go to jail. My kids need me." Cash yells at Nickle.

"It's here! You want to call it in?" Phillips asks.

"Wait!"

"Now why are you meeting up with the Mexicans?" Howard asks waiting on Nickle to reply. "Two's always better than one." He thinks.

"The Mexicans trying to take over the Bloods turf. We selling them information, in turn they give us information on who under investigation by the police." Nickle says reluctantly.

"Looks like they not telling you everything." Howard replies smiling.

"What do the Mexicans wanna know?" Phillips asks.

"We're not calling it in." Howard says straight forward.

"Now look we need informants, and you two already ready snitched so here's the deal we gonna let you go continue to provide information on what we want plus five hundred dollars a week or I'ma arrest you and let your homies as well as the Mexicans know you're both snitches."

❖   ❖   ❖

As Cash and Nickle leave, the driver in the blue sedan continues taking pictures of agent Howard and his new partner and writing down everything he sees.

+ 63 +

CHAPTER 26

S ee this here?" Kathy says looking on both sides of the sidewalk, look at all the women wearing skimpy clothes, accepting money from men they obviously just met and the men leaning up against the store windows or their parked cars in the parking lot, smiling every time one of they hold gets handed some money, you can tell which ho works for which pimp by looking at which pimp smiles when a ho gets handed some money."

"This is what men think of us, we're just something pretty to make them money." Kathy tells Morgan, as they drive down the street.

"Like we have no value." Morgan thinks.

"They I think that's the only value we have is to make the money." Kathy says, disgusted.

"Why did you bring me here?" Morgan asks.

"So, you can see what it is man really think of us and if they think they can use us for their own gain, why can't we use them for ours?"

"You said in your letter to YJRC that you wanted to do undercover work that you wanted to get into the minds of the people committing the crime, that's to get to know them you had to get to know them not through interviews but by seeing them behind closed doors I think that's the way you put it."

"Kathy, I don't like men, especially people who make a living off of other people's misery who suffer from sexual abuse. I'm against human trafficking. I understand that some of these women are forced into selling their bodies, most of them do this because they choose to. The main people that I want to lock up or violent criminals and drug dealers because I think they have a big impact on our communities."

"I understand where you are coming from and the thing about undercover work is you'll be in a lot of different environments and different situations. One day you'll be assigned to gets next to a drug dealer, gets to know him or her and you may even come to really like them, but you will need to focus on your assignment, that's the arrest, and other times it'll be someone selling guns, these are the worst kind of people, some of them are really charismatic. You will see what we think of them before we get to know them is different from who they are once we get to know them, and it gets difficult sometimes to make the arrest. So, my advice is do what you need to do. Look at what happened to you and ask, do I want anybody to suffer, or can I set my emotions aside and make the arrest? If you can't make the decisions to set your emotions aside and make the rest, then maybe you're in the wrong line of work."

CHAPTER 27

SK, what's up bra?" Reese asks, walking in through the front door.

"Shit. What's up with you?"

"Look, Mike and Bobby tripping on you. I ain't hear it directly from them, they called DJ, told him they want him to introduce y'all. I guess they tripping on you running the hood and not breaking bread with all the money you makin."

"All the money I making? I only been out a week."

"I know this what I heard DJ tell Spook right after he hung up the phone. I'm just giving you a heads up."

"Good looking. Look while I was locked up, I had some ideas I wrote down and some of the homies about to organize the hood. We trying to see who all on board. I think you'll like what we about to do. Sed, Spook, Alex, C2, J-Smoke, all in."

"What y'all talkin about?" Reese asks, looking over his shoulder Sheryll, as she walks out of the bedroom into the shower.

"The organization called After Death Incorporated or A.D. INC. The purpose of it is to gain as much control over the illicit activities within our realm of influence and convert these funds into legitimate Enterprises. The organization itself is not to control each other but to help us stay focused on our goals, laying out a way for us to listen to each other and do not interfere with each other's work. One person selling dope not going to get involved with the homie selling guns, we all agree not to interfere but to build each other in turn that builds the organization. We all contribute, we all gain. Every person takes on a certain role and when they demonstrate that they can do good at that they can take on bigger roles."

"It's not always going to be fun and games, this is something you need to understand. Other people trying to do the same thing, they'll take the chance killing and dying for it, you got to have the same mindset but be smarter than them. Stay alive to enjoy the money and not get caught, if you do join my key advice is always maintained the Code of Silence. I emphasized that because I just got out and knowing that you can get life, that means the possibility of never coming home so you honestly need to consider, are you willing to take that risk. You need to weigh your options, just saying yeah to sound or look cool not the right kind of decisions. Make decisions you can live with, if you just want to sell weed, make money, fuck bitches, cool. As I said we all have a role to play, once you in you in, if you decide to walk away cool. We don't treat each other like shit and throw each other away. If you join you have accountability for your actions or inactions, you got to let us know if you out so we can find someone else to take your spot, let me know if you want to join and if so I'll get you a copy of the Constitution and how the organization works and what's expected of you. I know C2 would love to see you join, it's something to consider. I think you'll do good, ask for Mike and Bobby, I heard they tripping, there is nothing I can do about they feelings. On top of all that they weren't even born here, they moved here from somewhere else started a hood and then left. You, me, DJ, C2, hella people grew up here I never even met them, and they think they running shit. They sound stupid as fuck!"

"But 40 and then." Reese started to say.

"Yeah 40 and then know Mike and Bobby, they rock with them, that's why we are discussing who want to do what. We going to talk more, just give it some thought."

"I want in already I know that much. I like the idea of structure, that's something I can identify with it." Reese says. "Something I never got at home." Reese says shaking off the thought. "I know it'll work out, I see the vision in your words."

CHAPTER 28

DJ, what's up wit it?" SK asks. "I holla'd at Mike and Bobby, I told him you don't really fuck with phones but Bobby said he going to meet you there and your boy Kyle been blowing my phone up, I told him I'd let you know he been calling so…"

"Good looking bro. if he calls back just let him know I went by his mom's house, send some pictures to him along with some books, paper, in stamps. What's good with you though?"

"Same shit, just waiting to see how this shit pans out with Mike and Bobby. I'm not feeling 40's position, but he a good homie." DJ says.

"If it comes down to it you going to be able to knock 40 down? Cause if not I need to know now to have someone else do it."

"I'll do it if need be."

"Look I don't want you at the meeting. Just say you not taking no part in it only a few people know you're in, let's keep it that way."

"Look on C2 older and he might actually side with 40 so look, this is what I did, I put the paperwork on a scanner every did some of the shit on there, put C2 name on it so if he sides with 40, pass this paperwork around and send one to Kyle from a bunk address."

"You a cold nigga SK. You going to put fake paperwork out on bra." DJ asks, not too surprised.

"If he sides with 40, we going to have to knock that whole crew down. C2 and them not going to be at the meeting and if you can't get to him, we got to get him somehow, without jeopardizing the whole, plus whoever rides with him we got to do it without putting all of us on the line and niggas Kissimmee the profiles and I doing going to jump on them so quick without us getting hemmed up for it."

"I feel you but you a cold nigga for that."

CHAPTER 29

Bobby, you honestly think these little niggas really just going to pay up?" His brother asks sarcastically.

"Shit if they don't, they got the game fucked up. We started that hood, 40 with us letting us know what's going on out there so we still got that, them little niggas healthier eating we can expand that with what we doing out here."

"You really are stupid as fuck. Look how we think we not gonna let some Nigga tax us, let's alone some Niggas that ain't even been in the hood for years."

"Look you ain't got to do nothing so I don't know why you crying like a little bitch." Bobby pops off.

"If you was anyone else, I wouldn't keep talkin, you my little brother and despite what 40 talkin about these niggas not going to go for it that's all I'm saying. I be talkin to niggas and bitches out there too, they really about it just like anyone else. Because cautious, C2 fuck with 40 and it's obvious he not telling 40 everything and that's his boy."

CHAPTER 30

Look bitch, you holding up my money, I'm about tired of depending on my bottom bitches to pull all the weight. You my main bitch for a reason you supposed to show these bitches what's to do and how to do it, they doing more than you how that look? What would you do? What type of example is you setting and what type of example am I setting by allowing it? Get it together or go back to being a bottom bitch!"

"Let go of my arm." April says, yanking her while I'm away and walking towards the shopping center. "I need to get this nigga out my face if I'm a pull this off. I'm tired of letting these nasty ass niggas put they hands all over me, the last nigga had the nerve to lie and say them ain't shit stains in his drawers, like I don't know what shit stains are. Uggh!"

"Hey lil Ma!"

"Fuck you calling lil ma?" She snaps at the nigga, breaking her out of her thoughts. She sees a kid dressed like he's grown and looking hurt because she insulted his pride. "You're handsome but too young for me." She says as she walks off and a smile starts to form on his lips as his self-esteem renews.

"Excuse me, I've been standing here waiting for someone to take my order." She says to one of the cashier's, walking back and forth, looking dumb. "Excuse me, can I talk to your manager?"

"I'll be right there miss." Says the primpy 20-year-old, immediately forgetting her.

"Hi. I was wondering where you got your shoes from?"

"Do I know you? I apologize, just been having a bad day. Names April." April says, looking the young woman over, thinking she could get her to help her out.

"I understand no need to apologize I just got a thing for shoes."

"Oh. I'm sorry. I got them from a store in Frisco." April says, lying. "They were on sale and I had to have to have them. I didn't get your name."

"Letti." The girl says introducing herself.

"I haven't seen you around here before." April says, admiring the girl's brown eyes.

"No. I don't normally shop around here but thought I'd try something new, got hungry and ended up here. The food looks good but the service not so good I see."

"No, this service is horrible, but the food is good, the only reason I put up with it."

"Are you here with anybody?"

"No."

"Eat with me, I can use the company." April says, looking for an angle to help her on her scheme.

"Alright, try to remember the name of the store you got the shoes from I really need a pair of them." Letti lies, thinking those got to be the ugliest shoes she's overseen.

Chapter 31

S o, how are we going to do this?" Sed asks SK.

"When he get there, I'm going to get out the car, look around see if we are being set up, come back and post in the car with you until bra show up. When he get there I'm a hop out, walk up and dome bra."

"You not going to hear him out?"

"I heard all I need to hear. Pull over right here." SK says, hopping out of the passenger side and getting nervous.

As the car pulls to a stop along side of the train cars, SK tells Sed to keep a lookout as well.

Look good?" Sed asks, as SK walks up to the car.

"Yeah, everything is smooth. I ain't seen nothing, no bums or nothing we all clear. Bra should be here any minute."

"That him?"

"We bout to find out." SK says, popping back out the car.

"This lil nigga better not be on no bullshit, I give a fuck how young he is. Nigga act like he grown he can get it like he's grown." Bobby says to himself, grabbing the 38 special and getting out the car.

"SK, what's up with you lil nigga? Been hearing a lot of good things about you. Nice to..."

"BOOM!" The first bullet hits him in the midsection.

"BOOM, BOOM!" the bullets tear into his shoulder and chest, dropping Bobby to the dirt on his knees been balling up on his side.

"Fuck you and your fake smile." SK says wild Bobby looks on shocked. Standing directly over Bobby, SK pulls the trigger one more time hitting Bobby directly in the side of the head, splattering blood and brains all over his shoes and pants.

"Fuck." SK yells under his breath, mad at getting blood on himself, he kicks Bobby in the chest and walks off leaving the dead body on the ground as he takes his last breaths. He can smell the shit and piss come out as death comes on.

"Where I get so cold to start Killin?" SK asks himself as he walks back to the car and an image of him being helpless and not being able to defend himself as a kid, flashes in his head. "Never again" The narratively place reinforcing the coldness.

"Let's see how shit plays out." SK says getting in the car nervous and not wanting to show it.

"You think the homies going to rock?" Sed asks

"We going to find out. We already got most of the homies with us but Mike wasn't there, I'm not sure how that works if niggas gonna push with him."

Chapter 32

Damn that was good. What'd you say your name was again?"

"Teressa."

"How old do you say you is?"

"I'm 22 for the third time." She says, giggling as she says it.

"You are pretty. You still look kind of young but I'm so you not lying." The predator in Tre could care less if she was 22, knowing bitches and this profession lie all the time about their age for all sorts of reasons. "She a new face in that will bring in some good cash. April did good about damn time she get it together" He thinks.

"You ok?" Teressa asks.

"Yeah. You just woke me out of my thoughts that's all. So what brought you into this line of work?"

"I met April and she told me I could make money and have fun, that I'd be able to make enough to pay my way through college, so I asked her to introduce us and here I am." Teressa lies, wondering if April done doing what she set out to do.

"I do need to get going so I'll get out of your way and come over after school tomorrow and you can have a couple customers lined up."

"You can stay here. I'll take you to get your stuff and I'll drive you to school." Tre says, not not wanting to let her go that easy.

"I really got to go plus I got stuff to do at home."

"Call me tomorrow." Tre says, smacking Teressa on her ass as she walks past him.

"I hope April's long gone." she thinks.

Chapter 33

Monday the 16th

Kyle,

What's up with my bro? I hope all is well as can be, I know you can Vision me out here living, know that Vision not complete until you living the vision and you see yourself out here with us!

Your mom's doing good. Went by as you can see in the pics. Yeah of course she wants her baby boy out here, you got a lot of people out here that talk about you. I got at them and told them it's all good y'all keep his name alive but it don't mean no more than that if you just talkin. Write him send him some pics tell him yourself. Send him your number so he can holler at y'all it makes a world of difference if you put forth the effort those small actions made the world. I had to explain that, and I gave them your address so you should be getting a few more letters every week. If not fuck em.

I also sent you a couple of books you should be getting them soon along with some stamps, paper, envelopes, and one of the envelopes or greeting cards and postcards. I also sent you some reading material on cognitive behavioral therapy. Some shit on material dialectic and I'll send you some more shit on economics later. I really want to see you grasp this cognitive behavioral therapy, learn how to use it, I wouldn't send it to you if it wasn't good or didn't serve a purpose.

Cognitive behavioral therapy skills training workbook. What is CBT?

"Why this nigga send this? Got to be more than low mood or anxiety."

The CBT model emphasizes that it is not the situation that's causes the emotional distress that an individual experiences. CBT argues that it is the individual's interpretation or view of the event or situation which causes the emotional distress. CBT works by focusing on the negative thoughts and learning how to challenge them as well as learning how to change unhelpful behaviors.

"Knowin this nigga, he sending this for me to learn how to change behaviors. So, if I can get people to recognize why they say what they say I can change what they are saying to get them to change their behavior. People that say I can't have self-limiting beliefs and tend to not even try to accomplish, so they must have tried at one point or seeing someone else fill in adopted I can't. That was their interpretation of an event or situation. So, get them to recognize that then work on changing their narrative too. Let's try and see what happens and if they don't get it, hit him with another positive narrative that's what motivates the change to do. That's deep and simple, change the interpretation of the event.

Material dialectics, we don't just talk about materialism, the science and method of approach is dialectical materialism. This is because reality is not static, reality is constantly in the process of change, reality is made up of contradiction understand, dialectics is a word of Greek origin meaning, dealing with conflict, or opposing things or contradiction.

"Ok, this some good shit. He talked about this shit a lot in dealing with people and economics. People have internal conflicts that prevents them from changing Behavior. The world is an external conflict, but both can be changed. Once I understand both of these complex and that's they are always changing I can find a way to create the change I seek, that's what he been saying all this time, I should have listened a little more.

Economics. What is economics? The study of how scarce resources are allocated among competing uses. Das Kapital published in Germany in 1867, Karl Marx focused on the theory of surplus which he believed explained exploitation by capital.

Chapter 34

40- what you think about all this?" asks J-Smoke.

"Sup with it my nigga." 40 says, giving him some dap.

"I'm not sure what SK thinking about all this he a good homie truth be told I'm conflicted between Mike and Bobby, they found it this and I seen SK grow up all y'all really. I'd rather not see it happen really."

"I feel you from my point of view, SK fucks with you he don't even know Mike and Bobby shit a lot of us don't."

"What they talking about?" J-Smoke asks 40, referring to the rest of the homies across the street.

"They not talking about nothing, but you can always go ask them and see what they say." 40 responds, who'd been wondering the same thing but low-key scared to hear their responses. They been seeing him and hadn't said nothing to him. "Go holla."

"Sed, where SK at?" J-Smoke asks, walking up in greeting the homies.

"Shit, he on his way, probably be here in a minute."

"What 40 over there talkin about?" Cash asks.

"Nothin, being nervous, wondering why nobody talkin to him."

"He said that?"

"Nah, he ain't say it directly but you know as well as I do 80% of communication is nonverbal. Go over there and holla at him." J-Smoke says, not really liking his or Nickle's excuse for getting robbed. 'Why you at our hood meeting anyway?"

"It's good bra." Cash says, cutting Nickle off from saying something to J-Smoke, I'ma go. He's right, I'm not from here."

"You either Nickle, y'all on some other shit when your joined PRG, it's ain't about dissing y'all but this turf shit and it don't involve y'all."

"I feel y'all and I respect it because I do the same as you just did."

"Damn J-Smoke why you get at the older homies like that?" asks Red.

"Look bra you need to do shit like that to establish boundaries. They not a part of what we do or how we do it. They separated themselves from us and if for some reason we go to war with them why we want them to know how we operate?" This meeting for a reason, we don't ever let no outsider in on who we are or what we do, that includes your mom's, pops, brothers, sisters, girlfriends, they not part of the organization, they don't need to know. The shit we doing ain't legal let alone if yo bitch start fuckin with the enemigos, now they got info on us because you wanted to be cool and pillow talk or your girl gets mad at you and calls the cops on us."

"You right on that. I'ma heed them words." Red says, accepting the wisdom of the streets.

"Here comes Evil, Mak, Justin bet they don't say shit to us and go straight over there to 40. There go Doha too."

"Fuck them niggas." J-Smoke says loud enough for them to hear.

"Where C2 and them?" Slim asks.

"With some hot bitches outta town working on some shit, to legitimize some porn shit."

"Here come SK."

"40 sup with it G?"

"What's going on SK?" 40 asks.

"Hold up let the homies get here."

"Yup."

"What's up with y'all?" SK says greeting everybody.

"What's up wit it bro?" They greet in return.

"Waiting to see what SK and 40 talkin about."

"I was calling Bobby, he was supposed to be here I'm not sure why he's not here." 40 says to everyone.

"So what we doing then?" Slim asks.

"I'm sure SK already holla'd at y'all prior to this, some homies not feeling what SK talkin about, they feel it's not his place. Shit, it is his place to speak his mind, them niggas ain't even show up to a hood meeting that directly involves them. What type of shit is that? As far as I'm concerned, fuck them niggas! What's your opinion ass for what SK talkin about or Bobby and Mike not coming to address the situation?" J-Smoke asks, "What's your position on this, is you with structuring the hood or you standing with Mike and Bobby and trying to tax the homies?" J-Smoke directs his question to 40 and the few people pushing with him.

"They ain't even show up." Doha says to 40, "Why we gonna push for some niggas that ain't even going to push for what they started?"

"So you with Mike and Bobby if they would have come?" SK asks Doha.

"You too 40?" SK asks.

"We with them. You not running this hood."

"BOOM!!"

"It's like that?" 40 asks Slim, as he pulls out in AK-47 and aims it at their circle.

"It's like that." Slim says.

"You shot the homie for speaking his mind." 40 says to Red

"He spoke the wrong mind." Red says.

"If you think we going to go against the homie for you? You got the game twisted, we all wit SK on this, Bobby ain't show up for a reason. You think we going to let some niggas we don't know come in and tax us, you really stupid! And you wonder why nobody fuck with you but these sucka ass niggas." Red says heatedly, ready to kill 40.

"40 you the homie, you too Mak, Evil, Justin, all y'all. We going to let your walk away if you're not wit it. If your walk away don't acknowledge this as your hood. If you in, you under this script." SK says to 40 and everyone with him.

"We out bra." Evil says.

"CLACK, CLACK, CLACK, CLACK..." The AK bursts, killing Evil on impact, hitting him in the chest, stomach, and collarbone, ripping through his back and spraying blood everywhere, one hits 40 and his shoulder. More bullets come and hit Justin in his back as he turns to run, gun in hand. SK walks up and shoots 40 twice in the back as he stands there hunched over holding his shoulder.

"Damn!" J-Smoke says, " I didn't think it was going to end the way it did."

"Shit changed when Doha bitch ass spoke his mind. Tax us, nigga sound stupid as fuck." Red says out loud.

"What about this nigga Mike not showing up?" J-Smoke asks.

"I asked cuz if somebody need to get him?"

"Shit. I'm not trippin on Mike but if you want to go, go. Ain't nobody going to tell you not to." SK replies.

"Let's get out of here before the police start showing up." Slim says, looking around, starting to look nervous.

CHAPTER 35

"Well, she obviously not yo mom, So tell me why you brought the white woman." Tre asks, still suspicious of her since April brought her around then took his money and left. "April's a smart girl so Teressa really didn't know." He thinks.

"She's my friend." Teressa says, looking back at her friend in the car while she does her lips in the mirror.

"Aight." Tre says, agreeing to meet her.

Teressa waves her hand for her friend to come over. "This is Lynn" Teressa introduces them.

"So you..."

"Let me stop you right there." Lynn says, cutting Tre off. "I really don't think you know what you got yourself into." She says, showing her badge.

"Bitch! What the fuck is this? Bitch you rots the police?"

"You done." Lynn interjects.

"I ain't got shit to say to you." Tre says, making a scene is he gets up to leave.

"Sit down and shut up or I'ma book your child molester ass for sleeping with and conspiracy to pimp minor!"

"Bitch. I am sleep with no minor!"

"Teressa is 16 years old."

"Fuck " Tre says as all the air goes out of him. "Why you lie about your age?" He asks, looking sick and defeated.

"I could if you died in prison." Teressa thinks.

"Look, I didn't know anything about my friend meeting you. She is only 16 that's not close to 18."

"Like I said I ain't know she was 16." Tre says trying to fend off whatever her angle is, because if she was going to arrest him, she would have already. "If you lied about your age, you probably lied about your name too. So, what's your real name?" He asks, knowing she's not going to tell him.

"Morgan, that's my real name."

Kathy looks shocked then angry at Morgan giving real name.

"Shit. I am thinking of going to give me your real name. It was a rhetorical question, surprised the fuck outta me. Any more surprises?"

"You're will it be a confidential informant." Kathy says.

"Fuck off." Tre says, trying to regain his composure and get up to leave.

"Or go to jail like I said. You'll need protective custody, and you know you won't last long on the streets as soon as everyone you know finds out what you are busted for and that you went P.C. so make your decision."

"Look, let me ask you first what you want information on. I might not be able to get it but I can pay you off." He says, trying to find out who they want info on so each and let whoever know.

"Your hoes or on the street '1417 sleeping with different people, hearing different things you are going to direct them where we tell you to and give us the information that we want.'

"Nah. He'll nah. My hoes will leave me."

"I'll leave your ass in jail."

Tre looks at Morgan with venom in his eyes.

"Eyes over here." Kathy says, seeing the hate all over his face.

"I need to figure a way out of this without being a snitch or CI." Tre thinks.

"Who do you want info on?"

"Never thought you'd ask. I need info on a person that goes by the name SK."

"SK" Morgan thinks, having conflicting thoughts of telling Kathy who he is and not, still mad at him for not being there and for being a criminal.

"SK? Never heard of him." Tre says, lying, not wanting nothing to do with him. "You got a real name?"

"No. We need his real name. All I have is conversations about him. He's Young and the shootings that took place on March 5th is the results of a power struggle. We're trying to figure out who was involved and what is the power struggle over and I can't tell you where that information came from so don't ask."

"I heard the same shit from my hoes." Tre thinks jealously.

"We also want to know who selling all the heroin. People keep overdosing."

"I don't know the dope game." Tre says, arms out and an opening gesture to say I'm not lying.

"Yes, you do. April told Morgan everything." Kathy says, still irritated at Morgan for giving this piece of shit real name.

"You got me there." He says, forgetting all about April getting mad all over again as soon as his narrative starts to replay and being reminded of violation of his own code. "Never trust a bitch."

"Look, I'll get you the information under one condition."

"What's that?" Kathy asks.

"You the police so you can look people up. You want April. Give me all the info you got."

"No deal." Morgan says.

"Then no deal. You can take me to jail."

"If that's what you want. I'll show everybody this video from my cell phone. That you are willing to snitch." Morgan says.

"What the fuck?" Kathy thinks, shocked. "I need to pay serious attention to this bitch."

"I'll get you the info." Tre says, sick.

"Start producing credible information within the next week are you will be sitting in protective custody." Kathy says disgusted.

❖   ❖   ❖

"What the fuck was all that about?"

"What?" Morgan asks.

"You recording the conversation."

"I didn't. It's just came to mind, I don't want to see no one get hurt." Morgan says, lying looking and sounding sincere.

"Oh, that was smart." Kathy says, at ease now. "Look, Morgan, I like you, you need to make some better decisions. You are only sixteen, you don't need to be doing stuff like that let alone sleeping with people." Kathy stops, not knowing where to take the conversation with all its complications.

"Kathy, I wants to ask, why didn't you tell Tre that's once he tells he'll have to testify. There is no such thing as an anonymous informant as the TV commercials promote, lying to the public."

"He probably I won't live a week once he testifies, and who cares he makes his living off the misery of others." She says, hoping those words at home. "Morgan, why did you do it?"

"Do what?"

"Come ears and meet Tre? Sleep with him?"

"I wanted to..."

"Get to know him." Kathy finishes sentence.

"Yes." Morgan says weakly.

❖   ❖   ❖

"So, it's official?" Reese asks.

"It's official." SK says to the group. "Me, Sed, Spook, Winch and Mets up with the Italians, the Russians, and a couple other groups. They support us in our decision to constitute our Hood, though I could have cared less to go received approval to be official in someone else's eyes. Some of the people I respect and got a lots of game from, told me, advised me I should say, to go this route, so we going by August 1st as the day of Incorporation."

"Why we doing that?" Reese asks confused.

"So there's no date to say our motives to incorporate involved killin the homies."

"Nah bra go with the date, that's official, we all put in to establish this I understand the need or Rank and all that and will respect it this and some things just need to be spoke on as a whole." Mizz says.

"What everybody think?" Sed asks

"3. 5." Reese says.

"3. 5." K-Bang says

"Everyone?" Sed asks.

"3. 5, it is then." SK says

"So we all in this together, everyone understand methods of recruiting and not interfering with each other and all that?" Red asks.

"Yep, it's all good." Mizz says, speaking for everybody.

Chapter 36

The police not going to give us twice a week to run our class. We can do it on our own during day room and study in the cell, so I got copies of the materials and lessons to study. Right now, I just want to share a few things with you to think and ponder on. This is some real shit that might make you uncomfortable to think on as well as challenge your beliefs, your thoughts, and ultimately your behavior.

"This is going to help you find your strengths and weaknesses. We young and think we know it all, can't tell me shit, all that good shit. I know I don't know it all, as much as I'm in here to teach and build. I am here to learn. Iron sharpens iron some people say. We are all fighting our own demons and don't even know how to name them, cause we haven't learned how to identify these demons. The first thing is to be open minded, the second thing we're going to do is learn emotional intelligence, identifying anger as a secondary emotion, remove our masks and be ourselves.

"We going to have to be honest with ourselves. I have pride but let me share this with you my first day here I cried. Being away from my family and friends, I felt in isolation I never felt before that shit terrified me, I needed answers to comfort me, as a kid we learn to cry because we can't talk yet, our parents Feed Us so we are. Crying to get what we want. This isn't that far off, I needed answers to comfort me, to help me with my feeling of helplessness. I cried unconsciously to get someone's attention to answer my questions."

"Thoughts, feeling, Behavior, the events that led so that's thought was being arrested, taken away, loss of my freedom, so it's event, thoughts, feeling, character defect, Behavior.

"Here is another example I want you to find your piece in the puzzle. Use a grid find your trauma or event, move forward in the progression of the event, you can change certain things to fit your situation. Here's an example, write down your narrative, what you told yourself when your trauma occurred what's character defect in the behavior strategies you adopted and when you starts to tell yourself your narrative, so if you doing better financially and you tell yourself, imma get it how I live, yo starts to identify that you are not comfortable financially or fuck this bitch when she don't answer the phone. Feelings of helplessness or whatever kicks in then the defect, cold, callous, manipulativeness kick in, then the behavior, robbery, using women, etc....

"The first quotes of the course is understanding you, why you do the shit you do. If this is the life you want to live or live it better. Chapter 2 is understanding your thoughts and challenging and replacing them. Chapter 3 is actions and new behaviors. Part two is material dialectics, understanding everything is in a constant state of change. Chords three is economics. Part 4 is organization and structure and ending with learning to give it away."

❖   ❖   ❖

"Damn bra, I never thought you were going to shut the fuck up." TJ says getting a few people to laugh. "My bad tile I didn't mean to hurt your feelings. Please don't cry." He added, being a smart ass.

"Fuck you!" Kyle says playfully, getting more people to laugh.

"It's some good shit. I'm definitely in."

"Me too." Mumbles says jokingly but serious.

"I want to get in on this material dialectics and economics shit you teaching. I think poverty my trauma, maybe you'll make me rich." Head says.

"So, start identifying your traumas and we'll go from there." Kyle says, handing out copies of the course and behavior grid, hoping to help people out and recruit others.

✦ 93 ✦

PART 3

CHAPTER 37

EVENT/ TRAUMA abandonment:
neglect-
abuse-
sexual-
abuse-
poverty-
rejection-
racism-
ridicule-
isolation-
betrayal-

<u>FEELINGS/TRIGGERS</u>:
sad-
depressed-
helpless-
lonely-
embarrassed-
insecure-
hopeless-
distrustful-
fear-
anxious-

<u>NARRATIVE</u>:
people don't care-
world a fucked up place-
something's wrong with me-

<u>CHARACTER TRAIT/DEFECT</u>:
cold , callous-
selfish-
self-centered-
self absorbed-
disruptive-
attention seeking-
manipulative-
pleasure seeking-
obsessing-
arrogant-

BEHAVIOR STRATEGY:
murder-
join gang-
sell drugs-
pimp-
use women-
carry guns (gives power)
robbery-

UNMET NEED:
love
acceptance
money-

NEW STRATEGY:
(positive self talk/narrative)

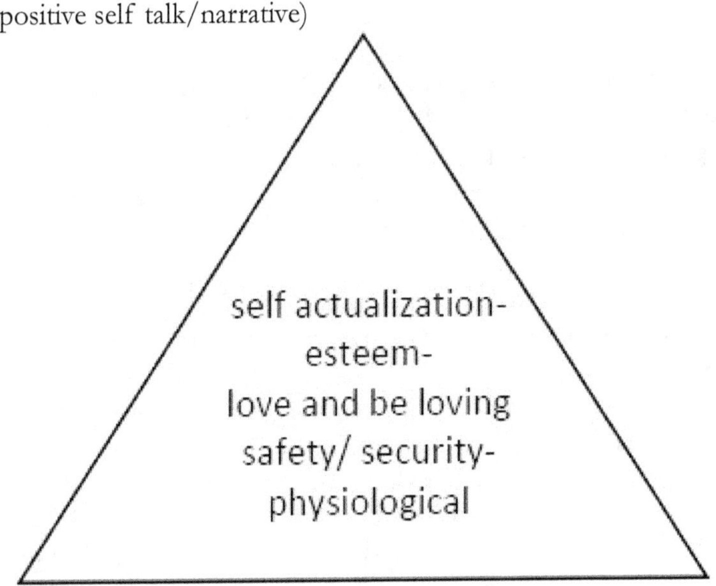

MASLOWS HIERARCHY OF NEEDS:

Chapter 38

What's going on with you? I'm Tommy Gunnz." The V dark skinned brother says, introducing himself.

"Kyle." Kyle replies, giving the brother some dap. "I just got here; I was in the halls. I turned 18 and they brought me here."

If you don't mind, what you busted for?

Two murders I ain't commit.

Damn, you started young." Tommy Gunz says

"It's a long story I maintain my innocence, I want to fight this and push for some changes in the laws. The way they doing me is wrong. They missing the original statements that took me away from the scene of the crime surveillance footage and replaced it with new statements. The video recording is just gone. I feel like a robot at times just talkin about it. The pigs tore my cell up and took all my paperwork. If I told you the half of it you'll think it was some kind of schizo conspiracy to lock up the next greatest football player."

Football?" TG blurted out.

'Yeah, I played football.

"Damn, I think I heard about you. You caught your case in Elk Grove. They accusing you of killing a Circle K cashier and some kid you played from the opposing team you played earlier that evening."

"Yeah, see you heard about it but that's me."

"Sorry to hear about that."

"I'm in on some real bullshit could have been gone or OR'd but I kept talking shit calling the fuckin pig a plan member "

"Why was they fuckin with you in the first place?"

"Shit. I needed some money so I can buy some food for my kid, I went to bust a check, the bitch told me to hold on, the whole time she went to call the police. I'm there waiting and the next thing you know I'm under arrest and because I kept talking, they brought me in, 2 days later I'm being charged for entering in occupied dwelling, kidnap, and robbery. I told the cops I gave a smoker 35 dollars for the check. I don't know nothing about no kidnap, or anyone being robbed. They fuckin with me because of the plan statement and the last just happened to be white, go figure, I call my baby mom tell her what happened about the added charged, she hang up on me, the next day I get an email telling me Kayla not mine but this nigga Smash. I been in here sick."

"Damn bro, that's deep. I know you'll be all right, you got to stay positive, that's the hard part, it gets easier, but shit, let me unwind, I've been on my feet all day I need to wash up and shit, then we'll catch back up."

CHAPTER 39

"I see your plan worked out." Wacko says to Rudy. "I don't know how you pulled it off, but you did. The blacks are at war with each other, getting locked up and don't even know why, freeing up whole sections in the city so now it's on me to uphold my end of the deal. You did a good job, and we commend you for that. All members agreed to your membership as you know you earned your way through blood, which you haven't done.

"Get rid of that look on your face, you came this far, it's already been discussed it's the only thing left for you to do, you showed us you have the ability to strategize, to be patient, and to execute your strategy to your desires goals but that's doesn't mean you are loyal to our cause."

"I'm loyal." Rudy whines.

"But you haven't demonstrated it." J-Dogg says. "You've only showed us you can't and we'll achieve something that benefits you, our cause is bigger than you."

"Here." Devil hands Rudy a gun with a big ass smile and says, "You've come a long way."

"Rudy, I don't think you know I was so see it as well as you think you do. We thought we did."

A confused look spreads across Devil's face, turning into worry.

"You told us the white Crip had smut on Devil for Devil to take care Ducc, we take care of the white crip, well we found out smut Crip Face had on him. He's been pulling over male prostitutes even minors and fuckin' 'em, one by the name of Lions, Crip Face cousin."

Everyone looked at Devil.

"He's lying. I got a girlfriend and a kid on the way!"

"BOOM!"

Rudy shoots Devil in the forehead, drop the gun and throws up.

Chapter 40

Big bro I called you the other day, no answer. I hope you take the time to slow down and keep your goals in mind. I'm not doing much, struggling with my attorney over trial strategy. Not sure when we'll actually go, I'm ready to push for a speedy trial, he says no. I tried to relieve him of my attorney on record but it's not that easy. The judge hit me with some legal standard bullshit during the Marsden hearing, asking me why I didn't want him to represent me. I clearly stated my attorney fails to investigate the missing video from the donut shop in the original statement from Dev White that's missing from the record, why my attorney doesn't have the original which he should have in the public defender's file. He refuses to give it to me, saying he gave me a copy already, which he did but the people came and took my property including my legal work. When I asked for a copy of my transcripts at that time, he gave me the second version of Dev White's statement, saying that's the one the D.A is going to use; How does he know the D.A.'s trial strategy?

"Long story short, the judge just asked my attorney if he's going to investigate my claims, my attorney said yes, so the judge said he's not going to relieve him. People say it's easy to fire an attorney, they must have never been through no real-life experience to speak on it. I'm glad I'm almost done with this paralegal course, have some more knowledge in this law. I'm tired of these fake jailhouse lawyers, they just as bad as public defenders and vice versa, it's just tiresome. I got a lot to talk to you about. Hope to hear from you soon.

Kyle

Chapter 41

Silver = eloquently persuasive
Fox = to trick by ingenuity or cunningly outwit
Silverfox = to outwit others through Ingenuity and being el-
oquently persuasive

"Bismillahhir-rahmanir-raheem"
"Al-hamdu lillahi rabbil alameen"
"ar rahmanir-raheem"
"maaliki yawmid-deen"
"iyyaaka nabudu was iyyaaka nastaeen"
"ihdinas siraatal mustaqeem"
"Siraatal-ladheena anamta alayhim gharil-maghdhuube alayhim"
"wa ladh dhaalleen"

Silver is a treasure because it has a high capacity for thermal
energy and conductivity, you my friend are a silver fox, you have

a way or should I say gift with words, you can out with a lot of people but Allah it's not a person

"Be careful, for what you are doing is dangerous."

"Brother Taliv."

"Hear Me out, you recite surah al-fatihah beautifully, we both know that's opening the surah in the Qur'an. What you are doing is dangerous let alone to bring it here. The doors you're opening or dangerous both with Allah and Men. I'll hear you out but only Allah can judge you and only Allah can forgive you.

"It's all I ask." SK says, "I typed this up and would like you and the brothers to read and re-read. It's the new Rifle Association one for everyone, all colors, all cultures and communities, we not only teach kids the importance of the Second Amendment but get them to understand the seriousness of guns, the impact they have in gang culture, criminal lifestyle, we want to bring literacy to people about guns and how they change lives when used with poor judgment. Not Just Guns are bad but how and why we use them makes them bad, that's the judgment, poor decision making.

"Yes, we seek to influence politics through financial banking, change some laws. A lot of abusive, oppressive, and excessive laws, hundreds of thousands of people cannot get good jobs based on being in possession of a gun or get people out on a 10-to-25-year gun enhancement. There is a lot of elements which are thoroughly broke down in here pact with psychology, laws, reasons for reform, and steps to take.

"What we're asking for is 4 you and the brothers to take a look at it and review it then let me know if you are on board to help fund this organization as well as stamp it as being good for the community, we want to see more Muslims in the city hall meetings, all walks and Creed's become assembly members and Senate members." SK finishes

"Brotha Ishmael mention this is what you wanted to talk about, he is right to call it's a warning. This is why I tell you to be careful, people like you typically don't succeed for a reason. They assassinate people like you for pushing this type of politic let alone law enforcement already wants you off the street, now you are bringing this into the equation, but I'll look at it and read it with the brothers, we'll go from there. Come back for Jummah. We'll talk after that but in my honest opinion, I can see you succeeding. Continue to share it with the right people, a lot of people will help you whether we do or don't. We will talk Friday.

"Shuurkran" SK says walking off.

"Shuukran" Taliv says to his back and praying for him while looking at the document in his hand. "He has a good Soul Allah, and I can see life's pain in his eyes. Let's that's our nothing else stop his success or he has a lot of good to offer the world, let others not slow him down but assist him.

Chapter 42

How you been Tre?" Kathy asks with an unpleasant smile. "I gave you everything you asked for I cannot get this dude SK name for nothing, give me a break. My bitches... Oh, you don't like the word bitches?" Tre asks, seeing the look on Kathy's face turn up at the mention of the word.

"Keep talking." Kathy says.

"My bitches my asking why I keep asking about SK, it's not a good look."

"I don't care how you look in street clothes or County oranges. Remember our deal, you can however much I don't like the word bitch, emphasize it all you want you're the one that broke it down and turned informant. Why you acting tough now. You are passive aggressive, That's some bitch ass shit. By the way, we got SK real name bitch!

'With got out of the way, what new info you got for me?

"I got a friend in the county jail named Kyle Grant; he's arrested for two murders he ain't commit. I got some real good info on SK, shit the feds might be interested in. I mean a lot of good info, all I'm asking this help my friend, he ain't commit those murders."

"What are you asking?"

"Something about a video from a donut shop that came up missing, I guess it would show that it wasn't Kyle who came out of the Circle K, not even who did. The fact his car was never even in the parking lot."

"I'll look into it. What's the Intel?"

"The reason for the shootings on March 5th was to incorporate, they killed the founding members and took over putting the whole Hood under a constitution called After Death Incorporated or A.D. I."

"Fuck!" Kathy says, surprised. "I heard about A.D.I, you mean to tell me SK is the founder?" Kathy asks rhetorically.

"That's what I'm saying."

"Can you find out who the founders are so we can get this fucker off the street?"

"I'll try. It's not easy getting info on they Circle, they real tight."

"How did you get this info? Never mind." Kathy says, waving her hand. "The beds will be interested in knowing about that and I'll see what I can do about your friend."

CHAPTER 43

"Tommy check this out, let me know what you think." Kyle says.

"What is it?"

"It's a behavior grid."

"Why you showing me this?"

"Something I'm composing, if you look at a specific event, say betrayal by someone you love and care about, you develop certain Character defects. Look at this grid, a lot of us literally sabotage ourselves with negative thoughts, those have an effect on us mentally, emotionally, spiritually, physically, then start using drugs to not feel zero state, that's the helplessness. We drive ourselves in circles trying to escape our demons. Those traumas ain't going nowhere. They'll be there when we go to sleep, when we wake up, when we sober up, when we get old and realize I did all this and I'm still dealing with these demons. I could have dealt with these then and now I'm old and just now learning to address all of this. The sooner you address it, the better head start you have. It's fucked up living a life of suppression and not knowing what's the driving force behind your actions is, you smoke dope to feel good because you don't want to feel helpless over some childhood trauma. All the shit you do is to not feel helpless, all you got to do is realize where it comes from, the feelings, the narrative, Character defects, Behavior strategy, address it and change the narrative how you view the events or trauma, and you can live a better life. Motivate yourself to find your life's purpose, tap into your talents and move forward, it don't make sense to wait until half your life is over then look back and say, "What the fuck was I thinking?" You got way more potential then bustin bad checks, themes could have been worse you could have ended up killing someone for some money to feed a kid that's not even yours and end up doing life. The kids going to eat, there's no need to do life you feel me?"

"Ima look at this, I know at the end of the day you going home in the world going to be a better place."

Chapter 44

"Hi, I'm Kathy, Elk Grove Police Department."

"Agent Howard, ATF. This is Agent Phillips FBI."

"I understand you have some info for us?" Howard asks.

"I called the FBI recording a person named Rubin Portillo AKA Skamz. I understand FBI is investigating and I was referred to you, so here we are." Kathy says.

"So, what's the info?" Phillips asks, irritated with this make of a woman.

"SK took over his hood by killing the founding members and constituting their Hood. That's the reason the shootings took place on March 5th."

"Ok. So, we looked into the backgrounds of the bodies that we recovered from the incident. We couldn't pinpoint any of them as being the founder of that hood. If you could help us with that, we could possibly have a case. What's the name of this organization?" Howard asks.

"After Death Incorporated or A.D.I." Kathy says as both Howard and Phillips look at each other.

"What was that look all about?" Kathy asks.

"A.D.I is involved in a lot more. Now we have a possible name to its founder." Howard replies.

"Look, my informant has a friend who is in the county jail fighting two murders he says that he didn't commit. I looked into the case, it looks like a lot of police and prosecutor misconduct going on. This is not my area of work really even area of concern. My informant has a simple request that's I look into a missing video from a store surveillance camera that would possibly show his friends car was not even in the parking lot, it was logged into evidence."

"It's missing." Phillips states.

"Yes." Kathy replies.

"Look, get us the names of the founders of this Hood that SK took over and we'll do you a better one. We'll have this kid cut loose on destruction of evidence." Phillips says.

Howard looks at Phillips then at Kathy. "The sooner the better." He says.

CHAPTER 45

D amn man. Life is crazy, I'm in here living with the person who was busted for two murders that I committed. He don't even know as bad as I want to speak up for him, I'm not ready to spend the rest of my life in prison. He don't deserve this shit at the same time, I can't stop crying. This bitch did me wrong. I can get out next week, kill this nigga and this bitch, write a note saying I committed the murders that Kyle is busted for and kill myself. Fuck! Kill myself? Only if I could talk to somebody. Kill the bitch I love, take the mother out of my baby's life, not even my kid. I got to do something to help this dude out." Tommy Gunnz thinks. "But what?"

Chapter 46

K yle wassup, young goon. I'm having a hard day bro. Drop some of those life with jewels on me." Ducc says.
"What's so hard?" Kyle asks

"My childhood friend told on me, got me up in this bitch fighting for my life. Shit fuckin with me. His bitch ass cousin up on the top tier, I want to kill his bitch ass, just so him and his family can feel my pain. I know he don't deserve it, I'm trying to rationalize it by the nigga being home on the Mainline."

"Ducc you on the right path. You recognize your hurt and trying to rationalize your feelings, that's what those two things are. Nobody told you to, if you did, to pull the trigger. Only you know what you did or why you did it. You can't change what happened. You can only change how you view it, accept it and change how you view it. What are you going to do to create a better future?"

"Tell me, what is the definition of a jewel?"

"Jewel, one that is highly esteemed, a precious stone."

"My interpretation is something that is precious or highly val-
ued." Ducc replies.

"Life is a jewel. Value it." Kyle says walking off.

Chapter 47

Fuck me, Fuck me, Fuuuuckk meee!! Oh my God. I love the way you fuck me. Don't ever stop fucking me. Stay inside of me. Cum inside of me." Morgan screams out.

"Damn Morgan. I love the feeling the way you squeeze my dick when I cum inside you. I can feel you massaging my dick to get all the nut out and you pulling my seed deeper inside of you."

"I hate you SK."

"Huh? Where the fuck that come from?"

"Where were you when I needed you?"

"Morgan, I care about you." SK says, as he lays beside her, bringing her closer to him and letting her head rest on his shoulder. I don't know what to say Morgan."

He thinks, "I know she don't like me being violent don't use that to reassure her."

"I care about you too SK. Sorry I said that, there's a lot I never told you or anybody outside of my mom and my sister. Nobody knows that I got pregnant, and I put the baby up for adoption."

Morgan says, shedding a tear. "It was just too much for me, then you not being around hurt me even more. I couldn't even stand the sound of your name." She says, covering his body with hers and crying.

❖　　　　❖　　　　❖

Surah 1:6
'Ihdinas siratal mustaqeem
'Ihdinas siratal mustaqeem
'Ihdinas siratal mustaqeem
'Ihdinas siratal mustaqeem
'Ihdinas siratal mustaqeem
'Ihdinas siratal mumustaqeem

"Guide us to the straight path. Allah every day I pray, I pray for spiritual guidance, for the wisdom to share with those I encounter that they may be uplifted in the way that leads to life in this world and the hereafter."

"Istaqfur Allah,
"Istaqfur Allah
"Istaqfur Allah
"Istaqfur Allah
"Istaqfur Allah
"Istaqfur Allah

"Allah forgive me for the wrongs I do, give me for those I hurt, only you can forgive and allow forgiveness into the hearts of others.
"Istaqfur Allah" SK says out loud to himself while Morgan sleeps at his side.

Chapter 48

Monday, July 1ˢᵗ

Kyle,
How you been? My apologies, I haven't written to you. Let me not make excuses, I just didn't take the time to write.

I've kept your address in my phone and saved some money for you. I seen Meeka's post about your current status. The things you are going through, especially with the missing video tape. I paid for a private investigator and she's an ex-paralegal to look into that. Hopefully that helps get you home as soon as she gets back to me, I will let you know the outcome. I gave her your attorney's name and number, not sure if she'll actually contact him or the Innocence Project. She's already not liking him based on Meeka's postings on this site. She got going for you. She got quite a following, so I am sure you don't need for in Pals or money.

There is a lot of stuff going on out here. It's not the same place you remember. It's grown a lot. A lots of our friends have unfortunately become addicted to one drug or another, it's very sad.

I did see your mom; she's selling t-shirts with your name and picture on them that say FREE KYLE in big ass letters with the website printed on it. I bought several and gave them away to a couple of tourists who asked about you after seeing you on the shirt. I think you may get a letter from the misses (smile). Like I said you are thought about.

I told the investigator to keep me updated every Wednesday, so I will write you another letter tomorrow and let you know what she says.

Much Luv,

TRE!

"That's a hell of a friend you got." Tommy Gunn's says. "You obviously got a lot of people who believe in you. I'm telling you keep on the path you on and you getting out."

"Thank you, bro. You have no idea how good that letter feels right now. Just someone else looking into my claims, I still got a little way to go, still waiting to hear from SK. He hired a paralegal for me to help write some of my own motions on Discovery, so all this is coming together, should produce some good results and hopefully I get this visit today or tomorrow."

"I'm anxious as fuck to get this busy and see what these people got to say."

"I see you wound up. You can't sit still." Tommy says, laughing.

"Fuck. What if they do find this video? This nigga don't even know I did this shit, they fuck around and arrest me, I do life. I need to hurry up and bail out. All this stuff this dude then did for me, he going to be hurt if I don't say something to him. I love him like a brother but, life."

CHAPTER 49

SK, I totally agree with you all the methods of distribution. I agree with you on almost everything, I just don't think we need to go to war over it. The Bloods are fighting over their turf with the Mexicans. We can supply the Bloods with guns and dope for cheap so they can drop the prices on the Mexicans and when more clientele, but if we robbed the Mexicans connect, it will bring us in they conflict. As in I statement, I don't think it's best to go to war with the Mexicans, we in the process of establishing not one but four organizations. We need all our members, look at what we got going." Reese says.

"We got hella homies and the Mexicans killing All Blacks that even go near they trap spots, they killing customers to, people are not feeling it." J-Smoke says, looking directly at Reese.

"We got the organization under control. We need more money to get this going, I mean actually fund the bank. We got financial backing, investors, board members, we got the economic development as well as the import export, and the gun advocacy group. Unfortunately to keep a game over the drug trade, a lot of people going to end up dead or in jail.

"SK, look we cook dope, we make and produce our own shit, LSD, meth, heroin. We make our own ammo and got licenses to manufacture or own guns. We can sell dope cheap as we want, the Mexicans will have to move just to make money." Reese continues.

"I hear you and I see you still learning." Says SK.

"They not just gonna move." J-Smoke says cutting SK off.

"So, what's the plan?" B Wax asks.

"The Mexicans getting they dope From the Sinaola cartel. They drop in LA. We got the who and where and when plus they getting it on consignment. So, it's going to hurt them because they going to have to pay that back before the cartel fronts them something of this amount again. It will set them way back. We going to chop the, take some OT, and drop the prices all across. That'll keep the Mexicans out the picture for a while. Eventually they'll push for pea treaties just to get back on their feet. We going to have to continue to push that connects away, severing all they ties. Use propaganda to push away day perspective recruits. They'll be out of here long before any peace treaty. When they do come for a treaty, we will let them see what our party line is, that we want their assistance but we are taking the role of vanguard and why. Then we can figure out a way to work together.

"Understand, there is no such thing as a peaceful resolution, this will also enjoin more to come to our aid." SK says, speaking to the group.

Chapter 50

D ucc, it's good to see you bro." Duce says, shedding a tear.
"It's good to see you too."
"How are you holding up in there? The food all right?"
"The food is trash P.B. and J two times a day, some type of cold soup, who knows what dinner is. If you look at the menu, they make that shit sound like a 5-star hotel serving you. Chicken ala 'keem touch of red pepper, side of fish. Shit ain't nothing but some dog throw up and that's not to get you to put money on my books."

"I feel you bro. I hate this shit. How are you doing otherwise?"

"I'm good, just waiting to see whatever happens. You seen that bitch ass nigga out there?" Ducc says, referring to Crip face.

"Nah. That nigga ain't been around, don't know where he been. Probably in witness protection or something, his mom house is empty and everything." Duce says, wanting to tell him but having conflicting thoughts of trusting him.

"Look, the Bloods and A.D. niggas linked up." Duce says.

"No shit." Ducc blurts out. "One update top dogs up in here with me. Nigga named... I don't want to say his name." Ducc says, remembering the conversation is recorded.

"They got a lot going on, feds all over them, something about a blood getting shot, a dude named, Short."

"Yeah." Ducc says, understanding exactly what Duce telling him, to watch his back. "Sounds like a lot of power struggles and new alliances being made." Ducc says.

"Powerful ones." Duce says with emphasis. "I'm a put a few dollars on your books so you can buy something and know what you actually eating."

"Aight bro. Thank you and thanks for the visit." He says, meaning, thank you for the warning.

"Love you bro. Stay safe." Duce says.

"Love you too." Ducc says, hanging up the phone and ending to visit.

Chapter 51

“Bluuuh, bluuuh, bluuuh!”

“That’s some sick shit.” Detective Navarro says, with spit still hanging over his lips.

“Yeah, that’s some nasty shit right there. First body?” Phillips asks.

“Yeah.” Navarro replies. “Any identification on him?”

“That’s why we’re here. Names Darren Snail, he raped a YJRC graduate by the name of Morgan Sanchez.”

“Don’t know her.” Navarro says.

“Her best friend growing up is a hot commodity, goes by Skamz.”

“Makes sense, think Skamz did this?” Navarro asks.

“Yep.” Howard says.

“So, dude into dismembering bodies and shit?” Navarro’s partner asks.

“This is probably a first but it’s personal. You can definitely see the rage.” Phillips says.

“Shit, I think that’s what made me throw up.” Navarro says, still sick.

CHAPTER 52

"Tre, what you got for me?" Cathy asks.

"Hi, can I take your order?" The waitress asks, walking up to the table.

'Yeah. I'd like two extra-large fries and two caramel shakes."

"I'll pass. Thank you." Kathy says.

"So, what did you learn about our friend, SK?" Kathy asks after the waitress walks off.

"When learned he's dealing a lot with the Bloods and the Muslims and he's orchestrating a lot of dope deals which I'm sure you already know about."

"Yes. You heard something along those lines, more suspicions and unconfirmed versions tell me about it."

"My understand you is he and his organization is pushing a black NRA."

"A black NRA?" Kathy says, cutting him off.

"Yeah, it's circulating around the mosques, they are looking for additional financial and political support. It's to educate people of all colors, nationalities, and coaches about gun violence in our communities and pushing for changes in laws for all the 10-to-25-year enhancements." Tre explains.

"I see there's a lot more to Skamz, he's very conscious but I'm sure the feds will like that. What's about him and the Bloods?"

"My understanding is and don't quote me on this, gay or lugging the bloods on dope and guns and the Bloods are helping them on some shooter shit but my understanding is they are helping the Bloods as well so the Bloods can have some it's done without it being tied back to them. I guess they had a meeting not too long ago with the 9800 Bloods and the 36th Street Bloods."

"Have you heard anything on the founding members of Skamz's neighborhood?" Kathy asks.

"No, not yet. I'll have something for you soon. My last bitch, excuse me, ask around, she came and told me that people were looking at her kind of crazy when she asked. She used to mess with from they hood."

"What's his name?" Kathy asks.

"I think she said his name is Cash."

"His real name?"

"I'll ask. Just give me some time, I'm on it. Anything on my friend Kyle?"

"Yes, very good news. The feds said you bring them the names of the founding members and they'll cut him loose on destruction of exculpatory evidence." Kathy says, seeing Tre light up.

"I'll get the names ASAP my friend doesn't deserve to be in there."

"I read his case, honestly I agree he doesn't deserve to be there." Kathy says, getting up to leave at the same time the waiter comes with Tre's food.

CHAPTER 53

Why Nations Fail". It discusses how one nation invades another nation, occupies that nation and exploits the Nation they're occupying. This book is by Daron Acemalou and Anthony Robinson. "Now look at this analogy, a rich person comes into the hood buys up the real estate in housing and business. Now you working for this person at minimum wage while the owner is making three to four times the profit, he or she is paying you. Now on top of that, there is an old banking practice called redlining, what this is and how it works is the banks deny mortgages and certain neighborhoods usually those with large black populations.

"The effect is to drive down housing prices which contributes to White flights, resulting in increasingly segregated cities. Now we're occupying these urban inner cities, working at their wages while they make all the profit.

"Redlining was actually prohibited by the 1968 Civil Rights Act; the effect is still in our communities, and we can see through political education. All they do is change a few names, but the practices are still the same, our neighborhoods in cultures are rich in different things and marketable.

"I can start a limited liability company for $159, 0 taxes, pay $30 a month for a virtual address and $20 a month for my website, offer stock, generate capital, and build on that. We will break all that down to specifics later business plans, Etc.

"What a lot of people do and I mean other cultures, Jewish, Chinese, Mexican, even more so Jewish and Chinese is teach deer children young about cultural values, political consciousness, financial literacy, mental and emotional literacy. They teach their kids the importance of each, to say it's not the same, that they haven't been through what we been through, ok. Chinese were banned to work for a private corporation by the California Constitution. Jews had the explosions, the Holocaust. Mexicans been beaten, raped, murdered, operation wetbacks, Mass deportations and the list goes on for all of us. My point is though through all that they stick together. How do we teach these literacies to each other and our children?

"Goal orientation. The first Revolution always begins with yourself, cultivate your morals, values, education. Tapping with your cultural roots, not the bullshit ideologies of get trunk when it get tough because it sounds cool on the radio.

A quick glimpse at that. Who are the major Distributors of alcohol, the major Distributors of music? Why is promoting, dumbing us down more mainstream than anything else? Who gains and who loses?

"The cultural roots I'm talkin' about that shape how we treat and respect each other, our elders, or women, our children, songs, quotes, Parables of wisdom that guide and uplift us to be the best we can be to ourselves, my families, our communities. These are the roots we wanted to get in touch with.

"Take a look at this, how commerce in towns contributed to the Improvement of the country. 3 elements, I'm going to the second element, the wealth acquired the inhabitants of cities was frequently employed in buying such lands as were to be sold. Take a look at that and reflect for a second on everything I said earlier. Now from the beginning. All of this is from a Wealth of Nations by Adam Smith. Number one, because they are afforded a market for its produce. Number two, Merchants box land and improved it. Number three, order, and good government were introduced.

"There are steps to it, it can be obtained, it can be handed down for Generations. As we work on ourselves, we make steady progress and attaining our goals. Now that that Foundation is laid, the next area of discipline is us: Ourself Revolution.

"I know we say it to ourselves, our kids, nieces, nephews; I'm a king, you are a queen. We're going to focus on understanding that and building interdependent relationships."

"Hey Kyle, where did you get this shit at? You got some serious Heat and I hear it. This is just the surface I know will get into all of it. I'd like to hear a little more on the king and queen. I'm about to go write a letter to my wife, I want to put some heat in there for her." Moon says.

"Aight, take a look at a king's or Queen's crown. The real crowns have 12 points at the top, each point which will go over later represents something. Those points represent a part of our character or characteristics to be attained, everything connects to building ourselves first then each other, then our communities.

"This is your homework. Look up codependent and interdependent. Now look at how these apply to relationships. When a person reaches dear self-actualization, they are 100%. Now you bring your full potential to a relationship, same with her. We'll go into that next week." Kyle says, closing the group lesson for the day.

"Grant. You got an attorney visit!" The sheriff yells over the intercom.

CHAPTER 54

"Babe, why do you do the stuff you do?" Morgan asks, wanting to know more about the man that she's falling in love with. "What type of husband and Dad would he be?" she wonders. "Honestly, I could rationalize in so many ways if that's what you want to hear or the truth." SK replies.

"Tell me the truth." She says, as she lays against him, hugging the blanket tight to her, feet stretched across the couch.

"I grew up with alcoholic parents, my dad was physically and mentally abusive and as a kid I didn't really know how to respond to it so I talked back as a defense mechanism which got me in more trouble and made me known as a troublemaker, which socially isolated me. Acting out and negative behaviors became a part of my makeup, it started to come more and more naturally. I gravitated towards other troublemakers and them to me which in turn led me to getting into more trouble. When I first held a gun, it gave me a sense of power I didn't have, I didn't feel helpless and when I talked people listened. There was also more respect.

Though I was already getting invited to parties, I started to get invited to a lot more. The more trouble I got into more accepted I was. my negative behaviors were being reinforced by social acceptance, office to make fast money, beautiful females, all this Hate My Life Style. Honestly, there's plenty of times where there were situations I would have preferred to talk my way through, talkin' about things wasn't socially acceptable violence is. That became my primary response and acceptance, APK my Primary Response whenever I feel helpless.

"If I start to feel helpless, I lash out. if I feel my acceptance is at risk I lash out. What that looks like, say somebody saying something disrespectful where if someone else hears or sees it or that person says I acted in a way that's not gangster and people in my circle would push me away. I'll fight to continue my acceptance with my homies even if I don't feel disrespected the thought of rejection pushes me to act out.

"I've been working on it, at first it was a process to identify the emotions associated with the traumas helpless to abuse, one, because I was emotionally illiterate. Two, because I was in denial about my feeling helpless. Once I understood my narratives like, fuck that ain't no one fitting to put they hands on me, I could feel my fist balled up. Short quick breaths, clenched jaw, squinty eyes, I realize here my Character defects start to kick in, cold, callous. I don't care about the next person anymore, then the assaultive behavior, fighting, shooting, pistol-whipping, do all that I've been working through it, untangling all that mess and building myself back up.

"Step by step plans really help me. I can measure my success. I justify my other actions of violence because of the lifestyle I live, where violence is accepted in talking things out isn't. I've come to realize most of us are honestly trauma patients, dealing with our mental and emotional problems, that's our basic social fabric. I know I won't live this all my life, I'm just using it as a strategy to meet my needs. I'll figure it out." So says, feeling comfortable with Morgan at his side falling asleep.

Chapter 55

Kyle Grant?"

"Yes." Kyle says, looking at the beautiful sister sitting across from him.

"I'm Karlie Champ. National Paralegal group. Rubin Portillo hired me to look into and investigate your claims."

"Yes. She told me about you and your qualifications, I just didn't think you were so young." Kyle says.

"I'll take that as a compliment. I'm 26. I started a paralegal course at 19, completed that, worked at a small law office as a secretary, learned my way over there now, my colleague saw that I have a good eye seen through bullshit, that's led me to focus my time on a system on Innocents cases, which I know you are. So, there's a few things I like to go over with you, what is getting you a new attorney, if you are interested, I'll file the motion for you, 2 is getting you a new private investigator to look into Dev White's statement, the missing video, fingerprint the shell casings, and see if there's a camera at the light where Watt was killed. Why that hasn't been done already raises a lot of flags, and the last who the fuck is Trevonn McCoy?"

"He is one of my friends. Why do you ask?" He replies, caught off guard by the venom in her voice.

"Have you talked to your attorney lately?"

"No. Not in 2 months, part of the reason that I want to fire him."

"I'm going to file for him to be relieved ASAP. I got a motion explaining in detail is ineffectiveness, a separate memorandum to go along with it. I'm sure Rubin doesn't know but your friend is a confidential informant working for Elk Grove homicide. And the FEDS or building a case against Rubin. I don't know all the details, I saw it in one of the reports, most of it is confidential I saw it's because, Trevonn is using his information to get you out. I'm not sure of any other terms and conditions but Trevonn is trying to get you out by providing information on Rubin. Anything that I should know?" Ms. Champ asks after delivering some crazy ass news. 'My friend is telling on my best friend to help get me out. Fuck!" Kyle blurts out.

"Why do you say fuck?"

"They're both showing me love to help get me out, I don't like or agree with Tre's tactics. Is love and support is there but I got to tell Rubin. Can you let Rubin know when you leave here?" Kyle asks.

"Yes. I'll call, I just wanted to talk to you first. Rubin wanted me to give this to you, it's some legal papers for you to sign. I'll be back next week to pick them up." Ms. Champ says, handing the papers to the sheriff.

"It's fine." The Sheriff says, flipping through the stack of papers, checking for Contraband before heading the material to Kyle while Ms. Champ stands up to leave.

"See you next week Kyle."

"See you." Kyle says to her back.

CHAPTER 56

"Skamz, young brotha. How the fuck you been?" Dirt asks.

"Good, and you?"

"I'm good bro."

"Skamz good to see you." Rhino says, giving SK a bearhug.

"Good to see you too." SK says, returning the hug.

"Skamz how the fuck are you?" Joe The Crow asks, handing SK a bottle of Bud Ice then walks up drunk to the next person.

"Hi. I'm Carla." The beautiful looking white girl says, introducing herself.

Holy shit! What's wrong with your teeth?" SK exclaims.

"Nothing." She replies, not hiding her all-black teeth. "I have gum disease."

"So, if I kiss you, I'm not going to get nothing am I? Like if I let you give me some head my dick not going to fall off for nothing is it?"

"No! Your dick is not going to fall off." She replies, laughing, liking SK.

"It's going to be a long night." SK says to Dirt.

Dirt laughs and says, "It's why I fuck with you, nasty motha-fucka." He Laughs Again and drinks from his beer.

Carla laughs again liking SK's easy approach.

"I need to talk to Dirt. I definitely want to kick it with you." SK tells her.

"Okay, I'll be over here." She says, pointing to a group of peo-ple hanging out on the sidewalk next to some bikes.

"Dirt, you want to call Jomo over or wait a few minutes?" SK asks.

"Jomo! Get that bitch off your lap and come sit on mine you foul smelling tramp." Dirt yells.

"Bikers." SK blurts out. "You mothafuckas is crazy. Jomo."

"SK. What's up brother?"

"So, what's the plan?" Dirt asks.

"This is what I got in mind but let me know so we can figure everything out." SK says

"A.D. Inc is still young and though we got a lot of good going for us, we still need to expand, we got a lot to offer, we bring two organizations together we can achieve a lot more. Your enemies become ours in our enemies become yours. We will teach you how to do a lot of shit, cook dope, manufacture guns. We got some crooked cops, judges, feds on our team. We can bring what you got together plus with the other organizations that back and support us, we can lock a lot of the black market down. Y'all roam everywhere which I like, it's in accordance with how we move. Guerilla warfare, one of our key principles. What we teach our members is how to cook dope even on the smallest scales, make fake IDs that's or legit as fuck, how to hotwire cars, job titles to get what they need. Everything you need to go under-ground, police tactics and how to counter police tactics.

"We have straightforward methods that are easy to adopt and that work. We don't do murder-for-hire except for political as-sassinations that Advance or agenda and those of our alliance. We need more members to help our organization. We recruit out of colleges, accountants, lawyers, bankers, got some new recruits out of the army, a couple in intelligence. We do weapons training, reconnaissance, we will teach you all of that. But most of your dope and guns come from us, help us take over certain territories and we will help you."

"That sounds good to me." Jomo says, smiling and thinking about the opportunity in the money and fun the lifestyle brings.

"Look, my main question is this and I came with this in mind. I know how fucking smart you are, all of the things you bringing to the table is perfect for us, we got what you want. You got what we want, it makes sense. My main question is this, will you help us right our Constitution?" Dirt asks.

"You wants me to co-author your Constitution?" SK asks surprised.

"Yes, help us so we can better manage our organization. I see and hear about your organization, how you move is real structured, for you to be so young and written your own Constitution and brought it to life, you got a cold fucking mind."

"Done." SK says, shaking Dirt and Jomo's hand.

"Stone, bring the camera over here." Dirt yells. "Take a picture of us. Jomo, come here."

As Dirt and SK stand next to each other holding each other's right hand and looking forward at the camera. Jomo stands next to them, beer in hand while the crowd of people watch. Stone snaps 3 pictures.

"That's going in the history books." Someone in the group says as the flash goes off again.

CHAPTER 57

So, what you think about these piece of shit ass cops?" Phillips asks Howard after listening to the wiretap they got on detective Moreno and Curt.

"Sick." Is all Howard can think to say.

"Very." Phillips says. "What do you think is the best approach to bring all this to a conclusion?"

"One, we got Curt talking to two minors ages 13 and 15, both adolescent males about sexual acts that have already been performed and soliciting asked to be performed. Two, we got Curt and Moreno on destruction of evidence on the Grant kid as well as extorting local drug dealers. Three, we got Kathy on shaking down her informants for money, we can cut her loose. Four, we need cash and Nickle or some other employment to provide us with the names of the founders of their organization so we can get Skamz off the streets.

"This shit with Curt, we can have one of our informant's leak information to one of the cartel members and extort Moreno. I could use a new boat. Let's work on number four, getting Skamz off the street." Philips suggest.

"Sounds good to me. I'd rather kill Curt and get a new boat."

CHAPTER 58

Juju!" J-Smoke says, greeting.

"Sup wit blood?" Juju says, shaking J-Smoke's hand.

"Same of shit bro. How you been?"

"Not bad. Could always be better."

"Twist this up." J-Smoke hands Juju some weed.

"Hi babe." Kristen says as she comes out the room and into the kitchen.

"Hi. Look, me and the homie need to talk if you don't mind, could you go to the store and grab some bacon?"

"Yeah, I guess, I'ma dropped by my mom's house then the store, about 30 minutes or so." Kristen says.

"That'll work." Juju says, relieved that she didn't start no fight or pop off with some rude ass comment.

"Y'all got a smooth relationship." J-Smoke says, admiring Kristen's character and looks. "Not the best-looking but it's not bad either." He thinks.

"She came a long ways, before she would have took that request as a form of rejection and started some shit."

"You know her pretty good to put a name to it." J-Smoke says, wanting to get to know his girl better.

"So, let's get to it." J-Smoke says, pulling out 5 lb of black. "It's 10 across the board. You can cut it to LBS for every 1 and it will still be gas or 3 for every 1. It will still be good, that's up to you."

"I'll take it. How long will you give me?" Juju asks.

"Fifty bands, 10 days." J-Smoke answers.

"Give Me 2 weeks, it's an extra four days but I'll have the money."

"That's good."

"What about this nigga Ducc?" Juju asks

"We got one of our lieutenants in County, he's working it out, should be done this week."

"How's shit looking with the Mexicans?" J-Smoke inquires about the turf problems that's been going on.

"It's all good, that shit dying down. They've been losing all across the board these past few weeks. Hopefully it stays that way because they cleared us out, literally took our turf and fucked us over. We didn't even see it coming, sneaky mothafuckas like cockroaches. They come in hard as fuck to get rid of. No matter how many times you bomb the crib. I think the shit you working on with the LA niggas that's will wipe out a lot of problems." Says Juju.

"I think so too. Do y'all need any more guns?" J-Smoke asks.

"We good for now, just keep me updated on Ducc and if you find anything out on Duce let me know." Juju says.

"I got you. Just run me $5, 000 for all five pounds. Drop your prices all the way down, $10 a gram or something. Start fluctuating the economy."

"Fasho blood. Good looking out on that." Juju says, shaking J-Smoke's hand as he gets up to leave.

"Be smooth blood." Juju says.

"You too bra."

Chapter 59

"Damn young bra. Why you tearing up the paperwork like that?" Tommy Gunnz asks. "Ooh shit! How the fuck you do that?" He asks, seeing the small ass cell phone hit the mattress. "This is not good news." Kyle says with a sick look on his face.

"What's wrong homie?" Tommy asks.

"Man, I gotta tap in and see what my folks talkin about, cuz honestly, I don't know but I know it's not good news. Can you give us some privacy?"

"Yeah. It's good bro." Tommy says, a little hurt at not being privileged enough to know what's going on. "If you need anything let me know." Tommy says, pulling the door jamb out and going out to the day room.

"Hey, it's Kyle, I need Skamz number." Kyle tells they homegirl.

"Hi. Nice to meet you."

"Shit, hold on I accidentally pressed something and turn the speakerphone on. All right I got it. Thank you. So, what's his number?"

❖   ❖   ❖

"Hello?"

"SK, it's Kyle."

"Kyle what's up bro? How the fuck you been?"

"Ready to come home." Kyle says, wanting to get straight to the point.

"Kyle, knowing you, you ready to get straight to the point so I'll get to it. We need you to knock down a crib named Ducc to lock in our alliance with the Bloods."

"I know exactly who you talkin about. I talk to him every day, he's in my economics class and was actually thinking about re-cruiting him, I guess that's out. Why he needs to go?"

"He killed one of Juju's cousins and they asked us to get him, so we negotiated a favor for a favor to solidify our alliances. We also Allied up with the dragon bikers, so you have that to work with as well."

"I see you busy out there."

"Yeah." SK says kind of at a loss for words, hating to have to ask this of Kyle.

"I'll get it done." Kyle says, disappointed in the request all the way around. "Have you talked to Karlie, the paralegal you hired for me?"

"No, she hasn't called me that I know of. Why what's up? Anything new?" SK asks, wondering if there's some new devel-opments that might get his brother out.

"It's pretty serious. This guy that I know, Trevonn McCoy tell-ing on you. I don't know what he saying or for how long he's been an informant, I just found out that he's giving up information on you to help me get out. I don't know how. I do know the feds are directly involved. Ms. Champ said she read it in some confiden-tial Discovery motion that was filed, she's putting in a motion to fire my attorney and private investigator. It's obvious they haven't been working for me. It's hard on me bro. I want to come home but not like that. Look bro, I got this address I'm going to give it to you, and I don't want to know nothing."

"I understand."

"Got a pen and paper?"

"Go ahead. Thank you for the heads up. I'm going to see what I can do to try and get you out, pay for another attorney on something. I'll talk to Karlie. Love you bro."

"Love you too." Kyle says, hanging up the phone.

Chapter 60

Cash. Nickle. Good afternoon to you, what's going on?" Phillips asks.

"What's going on? Why you have us come all the way out here to meet you?" Nickle asks.

"The I -5 is more efficient for getting around traffic and we need more privacy." Howard says.

"So, what's so important?" Nickle asks.

"We need to know who the founding members of you and Skamz hood is so we can build our case against him and hit him with the RICO Act on top of everything else, "Phillips says.

"Damn, it's getting big. I hate to see that. Skamz really a good dude."

"Yeah, a good dude that orders people killed, floods are streets, schools in communities with drugs and violence. Good dude." Howard says mockingly. "Oh, and he would kill you if he found out or should I say when he finds out you two are informants."

"I don't know who the founding members are. I left the gang because I was never really accepted. I wasn't privileged to a lot of shit that's why I joined the P.R.G." Cash says.

"I'm not sure, I was a nobody in the hood I was a Nobody Until I joined P.R.G. Nickle chips in.

"Damn I see you two got a whole lot of acceptance and self-esteem issues. We need that information, you two will have to testify. We will find a place for you in Witness Protection, so start making plans for your exit." Phillips says.

"We not going to testify." Cash says.

"Yes, you are." Howard says, showing Cash some pictures of him selling guns to P.R.G. enemies.

Chapter 61

Everything good?" Tommy Gunnz asks.

"Yes and no. It's complicated, I got to figure something out. Some shit I really don't want to do but I signed up for it.

I'm here if you need me.

"I really fuck with you. I might need some assistance." Kyle says.

Chapter 62

"Mom."

"Yes honey?" Monica answers her son.

"I love you." Nate says.

"Ooh, I love you too." Monica says, grabbing her son and hugging him.

"Mom, I don't want you to think anything of it because you know I love you and Dad. I know I'm adopted; I'd like to know who my real mom and dad are."

"Nate, we love you. Your dad and I talked about it a long time ago and made a decision that if and when you asked that we would do what we can on your behalf and of course, what's in your best interest. Your sense of belonging, your mental and emotional development and I do think some things are age appropriate. We will not lie to you or mislead you, but we won't discuss some details with you until you are older. Please respect our decision, we will always do what's in your best interest, that's the role and responsibility we took. It's out of love, what would you like to know that I might be able to answer right now?"

"Have you ever met my mom and dad? What do they look like? What are their real names?" Nate asks, fast and excited.

"Okay honey, slow down." Monica says lovingly. "We'll look them up on the internet and see what we can find."

"Type in Morgan Sanchez, Elk Grove, California." Monica says.

"Mom, is that her?" Nate asks, looking up at his mom.

"It sure is babe, you have some of her features, especially her soft eyes."

"Mom, she doesn't live far from here. Look it's like five streets away." Nate yells excitedly.

"Babe, it is possibly too soon to reach out to her. Let your dad and I discuss it first and quite possibly we can't reach out to her and let her know we live around the corner. Give us some time, okay?" Monica says, seeing the excitement in the determination in her son to meet his biological mom.

"Can we look up my dad?" Nate says almost yelling with excitement.

"Yes babe, just remember what we talked about give us some time okay?"

"Okay mom." Nate says while his mom plants a kiss on top of his head.

"Type in Darren Snail, Elk Grove, California."

"Mom, look that's him. We almost look identical." Nate exclaims.

"Yes, you do." Monica says, kind of surprised that the strong similarities, still surprised Morgan live so close to them. "Just remember what I said honey. Give it some time and we'll talk about it."

"Okay mom." Nate says, hugging his mom and falling asleep in her arms, tired from the burst of excitement.

CHAPTER 63

P lease state your name for the record." Nancy Juliani says to the group of individuals currently sitting before her and the Senate intelligence committee.

"Howard Steven, special agent, alcohol, tobacco, firearms and explosives."

"Phillips James, special agent, Federal Bureau of Investigations."

"Beau Alexa. Special agent, drug enforcement agency."

"Jackson John, special agent, Internal Revenue Service.

"Agatha, Bree, Homeland Security."

"Lovelady Kevin, special agent, internal affairs."

"Johnson Jason, Central Intelligence Agency."

"Luck Christi, Army intelligence."

"Moore Anthony, United States Customs."

"Rea Donald, Chief of Police, Sacramento California.

"All names are on record. I am Nancy Juliani, chairman for the Senate intelligence committee. The record is set to discuss some very problematic and disturbing news about several criminal organizations and their actions. I made prior to this committee that only one person will be giving a brief detailed report about the inquiries we have made regarding certain crime families and how best to combat with them. Let's begin." Nancy says, "Steven Howard, special agent, ATF and E."

"I'll be straight and to the point, our biggest concern is the Mexican cartels. They are flooding the state of California with unknown amounts of cocaine, heroin, and meth. They are also looking for American Guns which are turning up all over Mexico. Customs is flooded with shipping containers daily that's not including how much is actually getting through. The IRS is being flooded with fraudulent businesses that cost billions, there's a detailed report of the suspected crime families responsible for being major contributors and the rose they are playing.

"The CIA is receiving reports of terrorist threats and those reports include funding through these Enterprises. Homeland Security is having trouble separating some pseudo criminal organizations from terrorist organizations. They are so intertwined. Army intelligence reports high levels of corruption and misuse of Education in combat training. Their findings or relevant as there's high-ranking members of these organizations inside the Army and using it as a recruiting based on a small but global scale.

"The chief of police of Sacramento California also has some information about a new suspected terrorist organization which to the best of my knowledge is very accurate. I personally called him to attend this committee to speak about this new threat coming out of California. We have long Histories on the cartels, crime families on the east coast and detailed reports on combating them. Obviously, we are here to request permission and utilizing tactics to bring these criminal organizations so Justice and get the warrants that we need from federal judges and of course provide this committee with any information we didn't present.

"As usual, most of you know how these committees operate. We hear you out then read over the detailed reports and stamped the ones we find of concern which we do pretty quickly. On this new threat out of California." Nancy says with emphasis. "What do you have to say Mr. Rea and please speak up."

"We have an organization going by the name After Death Incorporated or A.D. Inc. they are actually a very young organization, their education, influence, and alliances as well as their intentions is worth giving note to. They have made strong alliances with the Italian mafia, Dragon Bikers club, the Bloods, Asian Mafia, Russians, tell you in a minute Arizona Mexican Mafia, the scary part is their recruiting methods are similar to the FEDS. They recruit mostly from colleges and the army. They work in groups or factions. They are already expanding to the Midwest and East Coast.

"One of the political ideologies they are pushing is a total front, it's an organization called G.A.G Gun Awareness Group, what is being called the black NRA. they are being sponsored by suspected terrorist organizations at the local mosque in Northern California, Arizona, Nevada, New York, and Florida. They are manufacturing drugs to help fund them, the founder Ruben Portillo has members with licenses to manufacture, sale, and export assault weapons."

"Excuse me Mr. Rea. I understand your concern. I, myself—I've seen this gag or ungag us and let us speak for ourselves You-Tube video. I actually love their concept; it is smart and a good thing for our kids and communities. Show me detailed reports of criminal activity, they're suspected drug-dealing and how it's tied into their legitimate foundations or something of that nature and I will do the rest of what you have to say."

"But!"

"No Mr. Rea this is an intelligence committee, bring me some intelligence and Mr. Howard, Ms. Beau will be replacing you as Speaker. That is all. Thank you."

CHAPTER 64

Nate, are you okay? You seem pretty preoccupied."

"No. I'm fine Liz Wesley."

"Okay, well let's continue. We'll finish this up then discuss next week's homework. Sixes.

6 times 1 is?"

"Six." Sara shouts out.

"Kids, please remember to raise your hands."

"Sorry Miss Wesley." Sara says blushing from embarrassment.

"6 times 2 is..."

"I found my mom and dad. This is cool, I still love my mom and dad, they raised me. Why did my real mom and dad give me away? I can't wait to ask. Will they be happy to meet me? Will they think I'm a good kid? I'll have four parents, 2 birthdays or maybe still just one. I can share with Josh. Will they really want to come to my birthdays? They did give me away. They will come. I'm old enough to walk home now so I can walk to Mommy

Morgan's house. She's not going to recognize me. Dad is too far. I just won't tell Mommy Monica..."

"6 times 8 is? Mate can you answer this one for me please?"

"48, Ms. Wesley."

"Thank you, Nate. Will you answer 6 times 9 for me?"

"54."

"And 6 times 10?"

"60."

"Well, we are done with the sixes. I think you kids already for sevens. What do you think?"

CHAPTER 65

"Kathy, I need to talk to you." Morgan says.

"What's going on?" Kathy asks a little irritated.

"Will you please just talk to me?" Morgan asks.

"Alright. What's wrong?" Kathy asks sincerely, seeing the worry on Morgan's face.

"Kathy I am scared. I never told you before, but I know SK."

"What? Why didn't you tell me before?" Kathy asks, pissed off.

"Because I was really hurt. He wasn't there to protect me when I got raped then instead of being there for me to support me after all that, he decides to assault the person who raped me and took himself out of my life."

"Fuck, I should have read the reports on that. His name has been right in front of me but I still wouldn't have known who he was at that time but I know his name now and could have made a lot of connections." Kathy thinks.

"Kathy, are you listening? I think I am in love with him."

"Huh? I don't understand." Kathy says.

"I've been seeing him for almost a year "

"Have you been sleeping together?"

"Yes."

"SMACK!"

"Kathy, I'm sorry!"

"Stupid bitch! You fine but you ain't nothing. Never going to be nothing. Stop crying!" Kathy yells, surprised that both hitting and verbally assaulting Morgan. "Morgan, give me a second. Let me calm down and stop making this about me. When you said you were sleeping with him, feelings of betrayal kicked in and I reacted. Sorry. Obviously, I still need to work on my past. Again, I'm sorry."

"Mm-hmm." Morgan replies, scared to talk.

"Morgan, you said you are scared. What are you scared of?" Kathy asks, walking back into the room.

"That he is going to walk back out of my life again. I mean look, even you are trying to arrest him. Two people that I love, one a cop, trying to arrest a criminal that I love and take him out of my life."

"Morgan I can see why you are concerned. Remember what I told you a long time ago, you meet people and start to care about them."

"I remember. If I can't make the arrest, I'm in the wrong line of work. Kathy, I need time to think."

"You mean take a break?"

"No. Time to think, evaluate my thoughts, emotional reasoning, why I'm making the decisions I'm making. Is SK meeting some unmatched need I haven't addressed, or do I really love him?"

"I understand Morgan and I am here for you, and I haven't said anything either because I'm scared to get hurt, heartbroken again. What you said really took me back to zero. I felt betrayed, my trust was violated. Everything I put into this relationship with you just crumbled. I am sorry I hit you and said what I said. It was to cover up the real feelings I felt. Obviously, I need to do some thinking as well because I should have never hit you or verbally belittle you. That tells me that I only scratched the surface of my trust and betrayal issues.

"I'm going to work on that regardless and I know it might not seem like the right time, but I think I'm in love with you Morgan." Kathy says as she slides down Morgan's body, kissing and licking the sweets wetness between her legs, all the while thinking how she can get her mind off SK and manipulate her to betray him so she can keep Morgan for herself. Arresting SK just took on a whole new meaning, Kathy thinks, Harry Morgan long as she places more kisses to the mound hidden behind the beautiful color of her pussy lips.

CHAPTER 66

Tommy, I need your help bro."

"What's up Kyle?" Tommy asks.

"I haven't said anything about what SK told me because I see you and Ducc are pretty tight but after watching you I see you not as tight as I originally thought."

"Well, what's up? What you trying to say bro?"

"I'm a lieutenant for A.D.I and the call to SK was about Ducc. He wants me to knock him down."

"You a lieutenant, surprised the hell out of me, all this time I thought you was a non-affiliate. Knock down Ducc though. What he do to get someone like SK to go through all that just to get him? If imma do what I think you are asking me to help you do I'ma need some more info before I make a decision on something like that. Like what exactly did he do, and besides helping you, what is in it for me?"

"Our organization has been making alliances with other organizations, one of those alliances is with the 36th Street Bloods, to lock that Alliance down we knock down Ducc and then they owe us one. In our organization we call it a Deadly Alliance. Only after death can a true Alliance be made. Financially, I can help you out, money, dope, guns. I honestly want to bring you in our organization. You got the game on fraud. I got people out there that specialize in it, and I think for what I got in mind you fit perfectly. What you think?"

"I got you bro. I respect it, the push in politics of A.D.I is what I live for. Let me know how you want to get Ducc. We can plan it right. The goal is to get out of jail, so we got to figure out how to pull it off. As for now I'ma spend more time around him so he gets more comfortable around me."

"Fasho! And as we go along, I'll game you on A.D.I., and we'll start putting together a crew for you and how best to get you established on what we doing as for the fraud."

CHAPTER 67

"Fuck that. Let's slide on them niggas." Nessio says as his homies discuss what just happened.

"Nessio, calm down. Look at what just happened. We need to look into the facts, evaluated then make a decision, not just ride. That could lead us and the wrong direction and create enemies we don't need." Yogi says. "What are the facts that we have right now?" Yogi asks Tweet.

"We we're walking down the street to the store. Two cars pulled up alongside us, they hopped out, guns aimed at us, check our tattoos, seen we are Southsiders, pistol-whipped both of us, stop this out. They said, fuck scraps, this Hampton blood, we here and if we catch any of y'all around here we ain't given no more passes, we shooting up everything, moms, pops, Brothers, sisters, businesses, funerals, everything. They took our money, dope, shoes, and clothes. They left us bloody and naked."

"Did you see any of their tattoos? What were they driving? Did you recognize any of them?" Yogi asks.

"One had a big ass H on the right side of his face, that's the only one that stood out. Another dude had a crown above his right eyebrow. I don't know if that's a game that. One of the cars was a gold Buick Regal, the other was a black SS Impala. Other than that, I don't remember much else. Oh, and a 38 Special that did this to my face." Stomper says.

"Shit. Pretty clear to me, they making themselves known and want this territory." Triste says.

"My dad beat my mom and me when I was a kid. That abuse had me feeling helpless. I told myself anybody ever put they hands on me on somebody I love again I would kill em, and over time I became cold, callous. I started to carry a gun, that gave me a false sense of power but what just happened made me feel helpless all over again. That put me back in zero state. I'ma kill them niggers With or Without You. I joined a gang for a sense of protection in belonging because I didn't get that at home but I realize now that I don't need a gang. I know what I'm talkin about. You just want to talk, not ride and I see you can't protect me. I don't belong here where my voice doesn't matter.

"I'm not going to put my life on the line for a group that don't value my life. That's my paradigm shift on why I'm walking away. If you got a problem with it you can get it now because if I hear something said behind my back I'm coming back. Other than that, I wish you all the best." Temper says, limping out of the garage, leaving his ex-homies behind.

"Temper, I respected, and I know my decision is to ride with you. Yeah, they are looking for a way out but are scared to say it for fear of rejection and they false sense of respect and belonging. I'm a real mobster." Triste says, sweeping his arm in an arch to indicate all these cowards. "But I know what a paradigm shift is and zero state. I respected and imma ride regardless cuz this Turf is my income and I'm not going to let someone else run me out of here, especially after I lost my brother to this war with the 36th Street Bloods."

Temper nods at him and walks out, knowing that you made the right decision.

Chapter 68

Damn. It's been a long day. I still got to get in the shower and go meet SK. I hope he don't hate me. I haven't even told him I'm pregnant, let's alone everything else. Megan is driving me crazy about meeting a son I don't even know how to get a hold of. I gave the adoption agency my name for the adopting parents to reach out to me later. I'm still not sure if I'll ever be ready. I just said I'll always be open to a child's growth. I, I, I..." Morgan cries. "I need SK, I need to talk to him and let him know he needs to change, that's the feds and Kathy wants him off the streets. I need him, I don't know if I can take him going away again." Morgan thinks with tears in her eyes.

She looks up as she almost wrecks her car, she straightens out her car and stops in the middle of the street as the little boy looks up, he locks eyes with his mom for the first time in his life and runs. "What the fuck. Why did that little boy remind of Darren? I need to really focus on what's going on in my thoughts. I'm losing it."

"Fuck!" Morgan says, out loud, still gathering her thoughts.

CHAPTER 69

SK, look bro. It's Cash. There's a lots and I need to talk to you in about, it's important, I've been calling so I can talk to you and meet up with you in person. I'm going to run so I have to leave this voicemail. I've been working for the feds, me, and Nickle, we are federal informants. The feds are coming after you. I can't do that to you. You really are a good person. I love your push to help others, it motivates me to be and do more for myself, my family, my community, the feds want to know who the founding members of our original organization or before you took over. Honestly, it's only a matter of time before they linked the pieces together. Nickle said he didn't know who they were either. You know we know, we both denied it. They told us they going to make us testify. I refuse to help these people destroy what you building.

"Your advocacy is needed in our cities for our youth. I hope this buys you some time to continue to build and build your path to be well-established. I rather be known for a snitch then they snitch who helped it bring you down. I wish I never took the easy way out, but I did. I apologize. I don't know about Nickle, but I wish you the best." Cash says.

He throws the cell phone in the trash can, gets in his new car and heads to the destination in Mexico. "I hope I make it."

CHAPTER 70

SK, Look bro it's Cash. There's a lot I need to talk to you about, it's important. I've been calling so I can talk to you and meet up with you in person I guess. I have to run so I have to leave this voicemail. I've been working for the feds me and Nickle..."

"Got damn it!" SK yells for the third time, replay the message. It's nothing but static after me and Nickle. "What the fuck does that mean?" SK says out loud, redialing Cash's numbers for the 20th time.

"Got damn it! Answer the phone!" SK yells, hitting the steering wheel out of frustration. "Fuck Nickle! I'ma kill his bitch ass. Least Cash has a fuckin conscious, he spoke up for a reason. Obviously to let me know the feds are on me and close. I should call the PRG and let them know to brace for whatever the feds got coming they way. Little Kentucky cash obviously running or suicide. Fuck it. Thanks for the heads-up bitch ass nigga-"

"Hello? Dragon. Look, this is Skamz. I just got a voicemail from Cash. He told me that he and Nickle both been working for the feds."

"They informants?" Dragon asks.

"That's exactly what Cash said."

"Fuck!" Dragon yells

"Yeah, I feel ya. I just thought I'd give you a heads up. I've been calling Cash to find out more. He left me a voicemail but after he tells me him and Nickle both are informants, it's nothing but static. Obviously, something going on and he's having a guilty conscience."

"Exactly. Fuck!" Dragon yells. "Thanks for the heads up. I got some calls to make. I'm off the phones for now. Thank you SK."

"No problem."

Chapter 71

"P erk. What you doing in there? Stop talking to yourself." Kyle says, walking past Perk's door.

"Shit. I'm the only one I get along with!" Perk yells out the side of his cell door.

"I'm in a real-life mental hospital." Kyle says, laughing at Perk's response, knowing it's true.

"What's going on?" O.G. Trell asks.

"Shit about to jump in the shower and head back to the cell and get ready for this attorney visit."

"That's what's up Young Blood. Good news I hope."

"I hope so too." Kyle says, getting in the shower.

"What's going on Tommy Gunnz?" Ducc asks.

"Look bro, I need to let you know what's going on. My celly is a lieutenant After Death Incorporated."

"No shit. You sure?" Ducc asks.

"Positive. SK sent this nigga a cell phone and told him to knock you down Alliance with the 36th Street Bloods."

"No shit. Duce came and visited me a while back and gave me a heads up. I didn't know his rank but I knew he one of the top dogs. So they linking up and I'm the target huh?" Ducc laughs.

"Kyle wants to make me a member of A.D.I."

"So, he wants you to help him kill me?"

"Yep." He don't know I'm already a part of an organization so this is my idea. I'm a joint date organization as a sleeper so our organization can get the Intel and remain a sleeper. I'ma go back and give him some fake conversation about what we talked about."

"You and Monster get on Kyle. Get him fast. Imma run in and assist Kyle but by the time I get there make sure it's already too late. That way I stay good with A.D.I, like I did all I could, work my way up."

"All good with me. I'll let the homies know. Make sure you cleared to be a sleeper. It's fucked up I really like Kyle." Ducc says, genuinely hurt to have to kill Kyle.

"Kill or be killed. This is what I signed up for, no turning back now." Ducc's narratives start to play.

CHAPTER 72

I saw my mom. I saw my mom." Nate says over and over in his mind while playing video games with his older brother. He is fidgeting with excitement, waiting for his mom and dad to come home so they can hurry up and go to bed and he can sneak out and run to his mom's house. "I just got to be careful, I don't get caught out past my bedtime and get in trouble."

CHAPTER 73

Look, Ryan I don't give a fuck what you do or how you do it for that matter. Give me what I want that's $10,000 a month plus info on Skamz I'm going to put all your business out there. You of all people know what will happen to you in jail, for one, lose your family, probably get killed in prison. A cop, child molester, it won't go too well for you and you know it. So, get the money and we're cool. Oh, and everything you got on Skamz. My career is ready for a boost." agent Howard says.

"How the fuck am I going to get $10,000 a month?"

"Start shaking down some dope dealers, got a lot of them over on 36th where the war's been going on. Start there you sick piece of shit." Howard says, getting in his car and leaving Detective Ryan standing on the side of the street.

"Fuck! Moreno's got that kind of money. I can leak his address to one of the people he's investigating once they kill him, I can go to his storage, take the money and I'll make up some bogus intel on Skamz that's will ruin Howard's career. Fuck his career boost. I got to come up with some good shit to pull this off. It will help Skamz but I'll be free to continue to do me. Who's best to leak his address to? I know the Russians still mad about their dad. Yep. Fuck Moreno!" Ryan thinks.

CHAPTER 74

Rubin, this is Karlie Champ, I need to talk to you so you can be aware of some developments that involve you. Do you know a guy named Mark Hunter, AKA Nickle? Well, he seems to know you pretty well, said he used to be a member of your old neighborhood and some organization called the PRG. He got pulled over and became a federal informant, he got pulled over again 2 hours ago with some drugs now he's cutting a deal to testify that you killed both of the founding members of your hood to take over and constitutionalize your organization. I got the news from a reliable source inside the Department of Justice, figure something out quick I don't want to have to come visit you in jail."

CHAPTER 75

"Goodnight Nate. Goodnight Josh." Monica tells her two sweet boys, hugging both of them and not wanting to let go.

"Goodnight mom." Josh says weakly, barely awake.

"Goodnight Mom." Nate says, suppressing a fake yawn, ready to sneak out through the garage door into the backyard and into the adjoining neighborhood.

Chapter 76

"Go, go, go!"

"BOOM, BOOM!" The battering ram splinters the stucco around the metal door frame and bending the cheaply manufactured locks on the door inward, allowing the police to run in.

"Get down on the fucking ground!" The overweight cop yells at the little girl no more than 4 years old sitting on the carpet watching TV.

"Bitch, get on the ground!" The other cop yells at the teenage mom starting to get up off the couch as her daughter kicks, yells, screams, and bites the overweight cop.

"Mom!" The little girl yells.

"Clear in the back room!"

"Clear in the master room!"

"Clear in the garage!"

"Is there anyone else in the house ma'am?"

"Your stupid, fat friend just told you the house was clear. Lard fat! What don't you understand? How do you even have a job lard fat. I know clear means empty lard fat!"

"Look young lady."

"Fuck you lard fat!" The little girl yells.

"Where the fuck J-Smoke at bitch?" A dike looking cop yells.

"You a dude?" Amber asks the cop, evoking laughter from the other cops.

"Where the fuck is J-Smoke?" She asks again.

"Look what I found." One of the detectives shows the group of cops in the living room.

"That's about what $100,000 cash?" Sergeant Lawton asks, looking at the bag of money. "Nice day."

"Look you piece of shit. I'll report it to Internal Affairs that you kept evidence." Amber yells.

"You a snitch huh? Just like your boyfriend." The dike says and laughs.

"I hate you lard fats!" The little girl yells again.

"Look, I'll be honest with you, J-Smoke probably going to go away forever. You got a kid to take care of. I'll leave you the money just tell us where he is." Sergeant Lawton says.

"He's with some guy named Skamz "Amber says, thinking about her daughter and her future and the truth about why all the police are standing in her living room.

"No mommy! I hate you! No mommy, don't!"

"They should be back in about 20 minutes they just went to get some food."

"I hate you!" The little girl yells, crying.

"Take them and put them in the cruiser. Wait outside in call backup. Miss, what are they driving?"

"Two tone blue and silver Range Rover."

Chapter 77

Look bro, I'ma drop you off at my pet and you can drive my car back. Since we got to go by there anyway, we'll just do it like that." SK says to J-Smoke.

"It's all good bro, with everything that's going on, who is your main candidate to take your place?"

"You or Kyle. It's something I've given a lot of thought to. I'm choosing to be in the public eye, I don't need nor want any associations with too much criminal elements. We laid the foundation the next step is to finish framing the political landscape in the Public Image and to do that disassociating the criminal makeup on my end is politically necessary. We need the public support and Trust. That's going to take a lot of transparency on my end. If I didn't honestly believe that the only Revolution is a violent revolution, I never would have founded A.D.I, violence is unfortunately the only means for a real Revolution. I'm aware that the police, feds are going to try to assassinate my character through my past and past Associates."

"Your reason for disassociating."

"It's not going to be easy. I've been networking with a lot of banking and political figures to be the face for a lot of our party line, and I'll be in the front campaigning. Honestly, I wish we never had to start A.D.I."

"I understand where you coming from." J-Smoke says not wanting his friend to beat himself up for creating a destructive machine to achieve a bigger picture.

CHAPTER 78

So, what we gonna do about Ducc?" Tommy Gunnz asks.
"Shit I was hoping to ask you. I been looking. I haven't found no blind spots so, any ideas you got good with me."

"Look, when I went to court, I got an idea that will clear us both, Bug and L was talking about A.D. Inc, they both sympathizers."

"Sympathizers make good torpedoes." Kyle says, cutting Tommy off.

"We get both of them on medical line, so they'll be out during day room. They can get Ducc to give them a membership, clean our hands." Tommy says.

"Think they'll go for it?" Kyle asks.

"Definitely. Learn the power of sympathizers. People like that are willing to kill for acceptance."

"Aight. We do it your way." Kyle says, still optimistic"

"Holla at them as soon as you can." He finishes.

"I'ma holla at em soon as I go out with shower."

"Kyle should be dead long before Bugs and L even get medical ducat. Ducc don't even got to get his hands dirty. Tommy thinks.

CHAPTER 79

"Damn, I don't even recognize myself at times." Morgan says, looking in the mirror at the dark bags under her eyes. "At least I still got my ass." She thinks, admiring her naked body. "I can't even tell I'm pregnant. Ooh." Morgan moans, as a cold draft comes in from the open window getting her nipples hard. "I should close that window."

She puts on a long shirt, walks to the window and screams, seeing Darren. She grabs the gun off the dresser. She pulls the trigger, hitting him in the forehead through the window, she then Falls Face Forward hitting her head and knocking her out cold.

The police sirens wail in the background on their way to another crime scene.

CHAPTER 80

"Haa!" J-Smoke laughs, seeing the dope Fein pull up to the kid serving dope on the corner. He sees how green the kid is when he puts his hand through the passenger window to showcase his product. "He'll learn!"

"Heeyy!" The kid yells as the driver smacks the underside of the kid's hand, knocking all the dope out of his hand on to the seat and floorboard. The car speeds off."

"Bitch ass nigga! I'ma kill you next time I see you!" The kid yells as his friends laugh at him.

"What the fuck." J-Smoke says, seeing all the unmarked police cars around the corner from his house as he cruises by, he sees his baby mom in the backseat of the cop car with her face in her hands crying, his daughter looking out the window sees her dad and as they locked eyes tears fall down her cheeks and she shakes her head.

He cries, whispers, "I'm sorry babe." he lets the tears flow and drives off, wondering if you'll ever see his daughter again.

Chapter 81

"What the fuck is going on?" Cathy yells at the cops standing in the doorway. Hearing the calls come in over the radio and immediately recognizing the address as Morgan's, she speeds over there like a maniac.

"Look ma'am."

"I'm a undercover cop, you stupid fuck! This is my girlfriend's house." Kathy says, showing her badge to the pathetic looking cop whose clothes look just as tired as him. "What the fuck is going on?"

"Look, this is a homicide investigation."

"A what?" Kathy is taken back, cutting the female top off.

"We have a kid, maybe 9 years old, shot in the forehead in the backyard. We found the homeowner knocked out on the floor in front of the window where the boy was shot, gun in hand. We haven't gotten much out of her. she just keeps saying somebodies name over and over again. Nothing else." The female officer says.

"Whose name is she repeating?" Kathy asks.

"Darren."

"Fuck!" Is all Kathy can say. "Darren is the name of the piece of shit who raped her."

"I don't understand. This little boy raped her?" Ms. Fuentes asks.

"No. Let me talk to her." Kathy says.

"Come on I'll take you to her."

"I, I was in my bathroom, I got cold, went to close my window and he was just standing there. I don't even remember grabbing the gun."

"Morgan it wasn't Darren." Kathy says in a low sympathetic tone, letting Morgan digest the words.

"Who was it then?" Morgan asks, still not sure.

"Morgan., it was your son...I'm so sorry babe." Kathy says, remembering looking at the adoption papers, Darren's pictures from the internet and seeing the little boy. They look almost identical. Kathy thinks and cries while hugging Morgan, empathizing with all the pain.

Morgan suppresses the news and passes out screaming.

CHAPTER 82

"Salamu na staha ku wewe." SK says.

"Salamu na staha ku wewe ku." Askari returns the revolutionary greeting and respects.

"I'm out front." SK says.

"I'll be out there right now."

"This is a nice ride." Askari says, looking pleased at his friend's success. "You sure we should talk in here." He asks, seeing the OnStar button mounted on the ceiling of the range.

"It's good." SK says, "I had her gutted, all wires going to the OnStar and navigation removed. The radio is nothing but downloads, new cellphone in somebody else name. Plus, my Asian folks hooked the phone up, programmed it so it bounces off cell towers all over the place. Anytime a few tries to link a wiretap to it, the digital footprint or whatever the fuck he did, automatically changes. Number changes and everything, luckily, I haven't had to see if it works yet. I take his word for it.

"Damn, I knew you was on. Hook me up with your Asian folks. That shit made me feel like I'm in the 80s with technology."

"So where are we at with everything?" SK asks.

"In the next three days we'll be ready to move on the Mexicans, take the dope, cut it, split it and flip it. And the guns?" Askari asks.

"They'll be here later tonight or first thing in the morning. 3 crates of AR-15s, some handguns, and silencers."

"Arizona?" Askari asks.

"They showing us a lot of love." SK says not wanting to give him a direct answer. "Justin knows exactly what to drop off to you. He had to find a new route. Caltrans put up a lot of new cameras, plus he been being followed. Everything is good no hiccups on our end."

"It's all good. I'll see you in LA then." Askari says, shaking SK's hand and getting out of the range.

"I like this youngster." Askari thinks.

CHAPTER 83

"Istaqfur Allah!"

"Itdhinas siratel musteqeem!"

"Allah, please allow my good works to prevail. Keep me safe from shatan, most things are out of my control, but everything is within yours. On top of everything Allah im hurt. I love my friend; I know she's hurt, and I know deep down she loves me. Allow her to show it, let us grow old together. I don't need a thousand wives, just one love. That's the fruits I bear be sweet and nutritious, like an orange, pleasing to all senses and let the seeds bring forth even more fruit for generations to come. Shuukran Allah."

"Damn." SK says under his breath.

"Pull the car over." The cop Hills over the car's bullhorn.

"Fuck it!" SK says. "They gon have to catch me."

"He's driving eastbound." agent Howard says over the police radio. "Coming up on the 50 East Freeway."

"BOOM, BOOM, BOOM!"

"Fuck. What they shooting at me for?" SK says to himself as he continues to drive on 3 tires.

"BOOM, BOOM, BOOM!"

2 bullets shatter the back window, when slamming into the headrest of the passenger seat knocking off a piece of leather, another goes through the front windshield leaving a big ass hole and spider webbing the glass. The car slows down almost to a stop. "Fuck!" SK yells, grabs is Desert Eagle, jumps out the still moving SUV and starts running as his range crashes into another car. He hops a fence, ditches his gun in the roof gutter of someone's house and hops down. He gets tackled by an undercover cop that came from the opposite direction. He slams his face into the dry grass and cuffs him up.

"Nice run." Phillips says, "But you are supposed to be dead right now, still quite a ways between here and Jail, if not, I'm sure you'll figure it out when you see the charges against you."

CHAPTER 84

Live with Liz Gotfreed and Susan L. Good Morning America. We have plenty of news to get to in the first hour, computer tech giant Martin Kloss dies at age 88 sending the Dow down 200 points following the news of his death. Two massive hurricanes off the coast of Florida and news out of California that's a suspected terrorist leader arrested late last night after a wild Police Pursuit and we have Anna B performing live."

"Good morning viewers. First, I just want to say to those out in Florida be safe and get away from the coast. Those are some pretty scary looking hurricanes." Brian says. "I'd like to talk about this arrest of the suspected terrorist leader. I looked into it and didn't find anything noteworthy of calling him a terrorist. We have some reports from a senate intelligence committee where the chief of police spoke of this individual and in mid-sentence was cut off by Senate speaker Nancy Juliani and told to bring intelligence, not to mention she actually commended Mr. Portillo for his contributions to the community. We will continue to follow this story and keep you updated. Vai, how about you?"

"Well, it's too hot in California for me. Mid-90s all week and a hot summer shower moving in. Moving over into Arizona. Phoenix is already 110 degrees."

CHAPTER 85

Today as everyday, we are faced with trials big and small. Some are spiritually and some are worldly, I'd like to share this with you. In King David's Psalms he expressed his daily struggles and disappointments, yeah, she always turn back to God. He was a victorious person because of his strong conviction." Reverend Dean's says as his voice resonates across TVs and radios for everyone to hear.

"No Megan. I need to see Skamz, he deserves to know the truth." Morgan yells at her sister.

"Morgan, I don't think telling him you helped Kathy get information on him to help prosecute him will help!" Megan yells back.

"You don't know SK like I do. He will be hurt but he won't do anything to me, I know he loves me." Morgan says, losing wind and letting the tears flow from the night's events.

"Morgan, I know SK too. I know he loves you but still Morgan, be careful." Megan says with tears drenching her cheeks, not knowing what you think about everything and just wanting to lay in bed and cuddle with her sister, feel her love and affection. She hears the car door slam, the car starts, she knows her sister's destination is Sacramento County Jail, to tell the man she loves that she is sorry and she's going to stick by him. "You hear the Reverend preachin?" Kyle asks Tommy Gunnz. "Yeah, I hear him bro. Look out the window. You see the clouds rolling in?"

"Yeah, it's a trip, rain clouds in August, it's getting dark too. I wonder what other people in the world are doing. How many people are listening to Reverend Rodriguez right now?"

"I know after hearing this sermon. I wonder what God's got in store for me after all my trials and tribulations." Kyle says in deep contemplation.

"Today is August 21st A Day to Remember." Tommy Gunnz says, waiting to give the signal. "I wanted a way out of telling him the truth about what happened. Shit, he gave it to me." Tommy Gunnz thinks, justifying the betrayal of his friend

"The Lord will accomplish what concerns me. Psalms 138 verse 8. What does this mean?"

Reverend Rodriguez's voice it's Morgan's soul as she turns on her car radio, wondering how to tell SK she loves him with her whole being and she can help get him back out by exposing all the corrupt shit these police been doing to arrest him, thinking about all the records she's kept at conversations she's recorded with Kathy and Tre. "That's only a small part of it. We need him God." Morgan says, crying for her and her baby, wondering what Skamz is doing right now in this moment.

"What this means is, well first let's take a look at King David's life and prayers, we see a lot of adversity but that he overcame."

"Man, I need to hear this sermon over again." SK thinks, listening to the Reverend preach over the intercom speakers in the County's holding tank, looking at an O.G. cry from hearing the Reverend's truths."

"I want you to remember Job and know that the trial will last for a time."

The O.G. breaks down crying again, asking the Lord for forgiveness.

"Let's go to Isaiah 66. Judgment of the Nations, how will we know who's been rightfully judged, who succeeds in the pool doesn't, every day is a trial and those who do righteous deeds will. Read verse 22. Just as the new heavens and the new Earth by my power. So, your descendants in your name we endure."

"Amen." SK says feeling endurance in his soul like a fire that can't be quenched.

"That was some deep shit." Tommy Gunnz thinks. "Only the strong survive." He says out loud, signaling his index finger to let the brothers no to move on their target while he walks into the shower. I don't got to tell you because you know better I don't need to tell you.

As the rain starts to pour down on this hot August day. She feels renewed. "I know he will never stop loving me, loving us. He'll be hurt." She thinks as the rain starts to beat down on her windshield. "God, I know you let our love and our family endure."

"BAAMMM!" A diesel truck slams into the driver's side of Morgan's car, killing her instantly.

"Now we turn to Mark 14 verse 1 and 2. The chief priest and the teachers of the laws were looking for a way to arrest Jesus secretly and put him to death. Verse 2, we must not do it during the festival or the people might riot."

"Mmmm..." Kyle holds the pain in as it sears into his chest, back, arms, and head as the knives tear into him. He throws a wild punch, knocking Bugs to the ground. L stabs him in the back of the neck dropping Kyle instantly. L keeps stabbing him in the back and the breath goes out of him as the knife hits his lung. Kyle closes his eyes, unable to move any part of his body except his eyelids. He opens them again, not even feeling the knife plunging into him. He sees Bugs on the floor, waking up, locks eyes with him and Bugs sees the betrayal in Kyle's eyes, knowing Tommy Gunnz gonna pay for making this call.

"Look homie, there goes the fucking nigger Temper we was talking about, with the H on his face and there goes the Buick. Time for get back, have me looking stupid for not doing nothing. I'm about this life." Nessio says, wanting to be respected. "Call

Neto. Tell him to bring the choppaz ASAP." "Sometimes the Lord takes people out of our lives for a reason. We may not know the reason at that time, even though that wasn't what we wanted, it's God's design. How we perceive such things is what matters. Don't allow anything to paralyze your growth with God."

"Damn homie, turn that shit off. I'm tired of hearing all that God shit. We about to kill people, 666 shit right now." Nessio says, turning the cars radio off.

"Here come Neto."

"Looks like a little kids birthday party." Neto says.

"Remember what they said. They will kill our moms, dads, Brothers, and sisters. No remorse."

"CLICK-CLACK" Nessio loads the SKS, and Neto loads the Keltec 9mm

"I'll drive but I'm not shooting." Hitter says.

"Damn, bra. You eat all the mangoes?" H asks Dame jokingly.

"Look bro, it's about to rain. "Come on. Come on." H tells the kids, oblivious of the enemies across the street aiming guns directly at them.

As the first raindrop hits Nessio in the face, squeezes the trigger, letting the 223 rounds slide out the barrel. Neto follows suit, hitting everything including the pinata, sending candy flying everywhere, knocking over the barbecue pit and sending hot ashes into the living room of the house. Bullets rip through cars and windows. "Keep shooting!" Nessio yells, mad he ain't hit no one.

Hearing the sirens, Neto and Hitter bounce, while Nessio keeps shooting, seeing the house catch on fire from the hot barbecue ashes. He knows they won't get up to run, scared to get hit by a bullet. Nessio smiles, gets in his car, and drives off laughing, hearing the screams from people burning alive.

"Skamz, where you at? I've been trying to get ahold of you all morning."

"Justin made the drop a long time ago, I can't get a hold of J- smoke either. Y'all alright? We need you to hurry up."

❖   ❖   ❖

"Cut her open! Emergency C-section!" the ambulance driver yells.

"She's pregnant?" The nurse asks, "She's not even showing."

"What's her name?" The doctor yells.

"Morgan Sanchez. She was hit by a diesel truck that blew through a red light. He's in the ambulance behind, sobering up."

"Brothas and sistas, before I close, I want to read something to you from the Holy Quran. Surah 26, ash-shu-ara, meaning the poet first I read lyat 181. Give full measure and do not be of those who cause loss. And lyat 189; and they denied him. so, the punishment of the day of the black cloud seized him. Indeed, it was the punishment of a terrible day."

From the Author

Though this book is purely fictional, the traumas that people experience are real. I do my best in trying to capture the framework of thinking about your thinking and bring the reader to a level of awareness of why people do some of the things they do, whether it's you or someone else.

The psychology and therapeutic module or directly from books or other APA sources, whether I brought it to life in fictional characters is Up For Debate.

The political science is directly for my education in American government.

My goal in writing his book lies in educating the youth and getting others to do the same or better. I truly hope you enjoyed this book and part 2 will be available soon as possible with more in-depth psychology, political science, and business.

BlackAugustRevolution2019@gmail.com

www.ingramcontent.com/pod-product-compliance
Lightning Source LLC
Chambersburg PA
CBHW070536100726
47907CB00004B/1147